ISABEL'S DOUBLE

about the author

Kenneth Lillington's first children's book, a detective story, was published in 1957, and he followed it with several more novels for older children before turning his attention to one-act plays, of which he has now written and published some forty-five. He has also published anthologies on marriage and on cats. *Young Man of Morning*, a novel set against the background of classical Greece and the Persian Wars, grew from his having to teach ancient history to eleven-year-old boys and brought him back into the children's book world. He writes for both teenagers and younger children. Another of his novels for young adults, *Josephine*, was shortlisted for the 1990 Guardian Children's Fiction Award.

ISABEL'S DOUBLE

Kenneth Lillington

faber and faber

LONDON · BOSTON

First published in 1984
by Faber and Faber Limited
3 Queen Square London WC1N 3AU
This paperback edition first published in 1994

Printed in England by Clays Ltd, St Ives plc

© Kenneth Lillington, 1984

Kenneth Lillington is hereby identified as author of this work
in accordance with Section 77 of the Copyright, Designs
and Patents Act 1988

A CIP record for this book is available
from the British Library.

ISBN 0 571 17067 6

2 4 6 8 10 9 7 5 3 1

FOR ISABEL CHOAT

AUTHOR'S NOTE Two incidents in this book are supported, I cannot say with certainty by fact, but at least by family legend.

My eldest brother was taken prisoner on the Somme in 1918. My mother always insisted that, when this happened he appeared to her in a bedroom of our house in London, and spoke her name.

Both my mother and father claimed to have seen the apparition of a living person. This was my second brother, five years old at the time, and asleep upstairs. His image descended the stairs, they said, passed my father in the hall, and went towards my mother in the kitchen, where it disappeared in the light.

I must add that my parents were singularly truthful people, and not in the least interested in the supernatural, of which as a general rule they were rather sceptical.

Just after I had taken my O Levels, Mr Pargeter, my art teacher, said:

"What you need, Michael, is competition from people more talented than yourself. At present you're a big fish in a very small pond."

"Yes, I know," I said.

I hasten to add that he was talking about my drawing skills, not my all-round genius. I was pretty average at most subjects, but I usually came top in art.

"There's a summer school for young artists in a place called Newfield Abbey in Somerset," he went on. "They've sent us a notice about it. They suggest people who've done one year's art at A Level, but we could kid them that you're mildly precocious. Interested?"

"Yes, very."

"Four weeks." He showed me a brochure. "Costs a bit, as you see. How would your parents feel about it?"

"Glad to get shot of me, I expect."

Which was unfair, but it was true that my relationship with my parents had reached the tongue-tied stage.

"You can't blame them, can you?" said Mr Pargeter. "All right, let's look at the details."

It's on my conscience that my parents were tremendously nice about it, and even insisted on driving me down. I sat in the back, rather apprehensive about all this talent I was going to meet, and visualizing, for some reason, an army of David

7

Hockneys, all brilliant, sophisticated, and halfway through A Level. But it gladdened me when we drove into beautiful Somerset, and as for the village of Newfield itself, it was picture-book, the sort of place that American millionaires would like to transport, stone by stone, back to the States.

The Abbey was halfway up the hill that led out of the village, and we reached it in a procession of cars all going to the same place. As we crawled down the long drive which led to the Abbey, my father made one of those moves that make him a public embarrassment. He turned left, out of the line of cars, and drove down a narrow by-path into the depths of the woods.

"Alec, wherever are you going?"

"Short cut."

"But it says Strictly Private."

"Never mind that."

My mother gave up with a sigh that implied that we should probably get lost and prosecuted into the bargain, but it is a fact that my father has an uncanny sense of direction. He has the cheek of the devil, too, and would drive through a private house and up the stairs if it shortened the journey.

The path narrowed until leaves were brushing both sides of the car. It seemed about to dwindle to nothing. But my father's instinct had not failed him. At the narrowest point the path turned right and widened, and we could see the Abbey ahead, ours for the taking. Triumphantly, my father trod down, and the car surged forward.

Suddenly I yelled: "Mind that girl!"

My father jammed his foot on the brake and my mother was catapulted out of her sulks. My father swung round in a rage.

"Don't bawl like that! What girl?"

"Yes, I do wish you wouldn't do these things, Michael," said my mother testily. "What are you talking about? I didn't see any girl!"

8

"You nearly ran her over," I muttered.

"Well, where is she, then?"

And it was true, to my utter dumbfoundment, that there was no girl to be seen. We peered through the trees. Not a sign of one. But I *had* seen her. I could describe her. She wore a green print frock, she had a slinky figure and short, raven-black hair, and she wore black glasses as though she were blind.

"I did see her."

"Well, maybe you did," said my father. "A member of staff, perhaps. There's probably an outhouse or something in there. But there was no need to shout. You could have caused an accident."

He drove on, and then, because he didn't want to be cross with me just before we parted, he made one of his predictable jokes.

"Nice-looking bit of stuff, was she, Mike? Wishful thinking, perhaps?"

I acknowledged this with a very brief sickly smile: more of a twitch, really.

Newfield Abbey had been built in the thirteenth century, and I was willing to believe that its walls were eight feet thick. Since the time of Henry the Eighth it had been lost to the monks and had been lived in by a succession of aristocratic families, who had decorated it variously in their costly, mainly uncomfortable styles. You passed through huge oak doors into a panelled hall, where there was a hush like the tomb, or a high class tailor's, and you were faced by a great oak staircase. On each banister post was a carved bird of prey trampling a victim. A grandfather clock stood in the bend of the stairs, and oil paintings in gilt frames packed the landing wall. All very dark-brown-and-gold and sumptuous. The main hall, where the inaugural meeting of the course was held, was in the same style, grand and baronial, but

9

when we came to the classrooms and general working area, there was a change to trestle tables and benches and dingy distempered walls. I've never known a college that wasn't tatty on the inside.

The course was for both sexes, but the authorities were taking no chances. The girls were to sleep in rooms in the main building, and the boys in chalets a quarter of a mile down the drive. Possibly there were barbed wire fences at intervals, but I didn't think this was going to concern me much, because I was feeling lonely and inferior. As Mr Pargeter had said, the students were mostly older than I. The boys were better-looking and more sure of themselves, and all the girls seemed much more mature than I was: young women. Everyone got very chatty with everyone while I sat through the inaugural meeting and the evening meal without speaking to a soul. I went on to coffee in the lounge and sat nursing my cup and trying to look nonchalant, though it was a strain keeping my eyebrows raised.

And then the lounge door opened and the girl I had seen in the woods came in. I had not been mistaken. I recognized her at once: the stylishly-cut black hair, the expensive green frock, so different from the routine jeans and T-shirts of the other students. The only change was that she was no longer wearing black glasses, and obviously there was no question of her being blind. She was slight and willowy, with a pussy-cat face, and a general air of being able to attract attention without trying. Everyone looked round, and then all conversation stopped. She seemed to take this kind of reception for granted; she took a cup of coffee from the sideboard and found an empty chair, which, as it happened, was next to mine.

I found the courage to speak to her. "Hallo," I said, "did you get lost?"

"Sorry?"

"I mean, we didn't see you at dinner."

"No, I've only just arrived. I live quite near here."

Without thinking, I said, "But I saw you. In the woods this afternoon. Didn't I?"

She didn't answer for at least ten seconds. It was an offended silence. Then she said aggressively, "No, you didn't. I told you, I've only just arrived."

I didn't know what to say.

One of the male students, a smooth type, said, "If she'd been around, you don't think we wouldn't have noticed, do you?"

"Sorry," I said. "My mistake."

"Yes, it is your mistake," she said agitatedly. "I got here only a few minutes ago."

I looked at her face and saw that she had gone pale.

2 It would have been tactless to pursue the matter. I'd seen her all right, and she knew it. Still, it was no business of mine.

For the next day we were too busy settling in for me to speculate any more about her. They were cramming a lot into the course and we went from History of Art to Anatomy to working from a model without a pause, except shoulder-to-shoulder coffee in the morning. The working from a model caused a slight flutter of anticipation, because—to speak for the boys anyway—not many of us were used to contemplating naked females in the flesh at close range, but the flutter expired when we saw the model. She was solid and muscular and middle-aged, and looked so indifferent that we were chastened and all tried to look as professional as possible. She stood with one hand behind her head, the other arm stretched out to a reading desk on which she had a paperback propped up. Every now and then she turned a page with a neat flick of the finger. I spotted the cover; it showed a man with a bronzed torso of terrific muscularity embracing a pink-and-white girl in a crinoline. She read on, looking bored.

After a while the tutor drifted up behind me. I don't like being overlooked while I'm drawing, and it raised my pulse a bit, but he said:

"Yes, a good first attempt. You've got a good sense of form, but don't flatter her. Look, she has a peasant's body, heavy, rather ungainly. M'm?" (I was near the model and she could hear every word of this, but she showed no response whatsoever.) "Your drawing is too pretty for her. But keep trying. M'm?"

He strolled over to my girl-from-the-woods. Her name, I had learned, was Isabel Carrick. She seemed likely to keep it. She was marvellous-looking but extremely standoffish, and when spoken to either said "yes" or "no" or just walked away. The general impression was that she thought herself too good for us.

I watched her from the corner of my eye. If I had been nervous at being overlooked, she was much more so. As the tutor stood behind her, she tensed up so much that, if I'd shoved her off her seat, she'd have fallen rigid, without altering the position of her limbs. But he was impressed. "That's fine," he said. "That's *fine*," and put her in a glow. When he had gone, I risked a snub and tiptoed over to look at her drawing. It was very good, much better than mine. The lines were fewer, and firmer, and knew where they were going.

"Now that I've seen this," I said, "I shall stick to distempering walls."

She did not look round. "So you approve, do you?"

"Yes, I think it's terrific."

"Thank you."

I went back to my place. I had received my snub. I was a little red in the face. I didn't look round at her again and I avoided her at lunch in the canteen. My pride was hurt. To hell with her.

That afternoon we had our first lesson in water-colouring. By now I was feeling dejected and rather homesick, but the tutor was a tonic; a brisk, friendly girl of about twenty-five, very nice-looking, with tight brown curls and gorgeous green eyes and a smile that would have made the birds drop out of the trees. Her name was Jenny O'Brien. I sat in the front row, admiring her, and forgot about the exclusive Isabel, a couple of rows back.

She started off by giving us a few tips. "But," she said, "I can only really get going when I've seen what you can do, so I'm going to turn you loose this afternoon and let you paint me something. Look, I'm afraid this is rather like O Level essays, but I find that it helps to get people started." And she wrote up several subjects on the blackboard: A Seascape; A Winter Scene; Fire in the City, etc. "Or," she said, "by all means ignore these subjects and draw something of your own choice. O.K.?"

I sat thinking it over for a bit. Water-colour is a difficult medium; you can't paint over your mistakes, or rub them out, and your paint dries quickly, so before you can put it on paper you must be sure what you want to do. In the face of all this, I decided on something really hard. I decided to do a painting of Loneliness. Perhaps my present state of mind had something to do with it, but I didn't really believe that; the more I went on with my painting the more I felt that it wasn't my decision at all. I had the strangest feeling of being *guided* in what I was doing. There was nothing eerie about it; in fact it was rather reassuring, like driving in an instructor's car with dual control. But strange.

I painted a large garden, or small park, conveying the distant house and the trees with impressionistic dabs and aiming at deep perspective. In the forefront, gazing out through railings, I put the face of a small child. The face only, and so young that it might have been either a girl's or a boy's. Normally I hate sentimental pictures of children. They get their effects too cheaply. But this wasn't sentimental, this white smudge with the bars down it; was disturbing, it ached. You sensed that it was looking out at a world of other children from which it was cut off, like a bird in a cage. Though I say it myself, it was very good. I kept at it

14

all the afternoon. They brought us tea, but I let mine go cold. When at last I sat back, I found that I was tired out. I looked at my painting with wonder, feeling that I wasn't altogether responsible for it.

Jenny, like a good tutor, had left us alone while we worked, coming over only when a student asked for help. Now she began moving around among us, working from the back of the room, murmuring a few words of comment to each one as she went. At one point I heard her say "Ah!" and speak quite excitedly in her low voice, and I guessed without looking round that this had been caused by Isabel, who'd come top again, no doubt.

She came to me. "Well, well," she said. Then: "Do you two come from the same school?"

She meant me and Isabel. "We've never met before," I said.

"I thought you must have worked this over before," she said. "Well, is this a picture from some school art-book that you've copied from memory?"

"No!"

"Then it's a truly remarkable coincidence." She turned back to Isabel. "Would you bring yours over?"

"You see what I mean?" she said.

Yes. Isabel's painting and mine were identical. Hers was technically better, but the details were the same: the house, the trees, the ornamental lake, the railings, the child's face. You could have measured the distances between the objects in our two paintings and found them exactly the same.

"Well, don't look so worried," said Jenny. "This is rather amazing, but you haven't committed a crime."

I must have looked dismayed. But Isabel looked aghast.

I had made a few friends by now, and spent the evening in one of Newfield's pubs with them, but not very happily, because the coincidence of the two paintings fretted me. I was afraid that Jenny would somehow think less of me for it, in spite of her assurances, and it preyed on my mind so much that the next morning I caught her when she was reading some post in the hall and said, "Jenny, about those paintings. It *was* a coincidence. I swear I've never seen a picture like that before, and you can see that I couldn't have copied Isabel from where I was."

"Neither could she you," said Jenny, "unless she's got periscope eyes. Oh, don't worry, Michael. I'd forgotten it, really."

"It's very strange," I muttered.

"Oh, not really. If you'd ever run a painting competition, you'd know that you don't just get two paintings alike, you get hundreds."

"You don't believe in telepathy, Jenny?"

"No, I don't," she retorted with surprising sharpness. "And I'd advise you to get any such nonsense out of your head. Thinking on those lines can make you needlessly miserable."

"All right," I said, slightly startled.

She gave me her magnificent grin. "So that's telling you," she said.

"I think Isabel took it worse than I did," I said.

"Yes," said Jenny. "Yes, I'm afraid she did. Something's wrong, anyway. I'm afraid she's leaving us."

"What?"

"Look at this." She held out the letter she was reading.

"Dear Miss O'Brien,
I am afraid I have got to pack the course in. I am very disappointed, because I was enjoying it, and I liked your class and was looking forward to getting to know you better.

I shall be leaving tomorrow morning and probably won't see you again. I know that as my Course Tutor you will feel bound to follow this up, but please don't come after me and ask for explanations or try to persuade me to change my mind. There is no way of explaining this.

It has been really nice meeting you and I hope the rest of the course will go well.

With every good wish, yours sincerely, Isabel Carrick."

"God," I said.

"Yes, I'm sorry. She has a lot of talent. Had she become your girl friend, Michael?"

"Rather more like my girl foe."

"M'm," said Jenny, in a tone that suggested that the two might be compatible. "Oh, well. A rather difficult girl, it seemed to me?"

"I think she's got some sort of persecution complex."

"Do you? Why?"

"She gets uptight so easily."

"Yes. Dramatizes herself a bit. I'm not sure I'd like to share a flat with her. Oh, well. Sorry I barked just now."

No, Isabel was assuredly not my girl friend, but all the same, I was much more upset at the thought of her leaving than I had any reason to be. I spent the morning taking continual glances at doors in the hope that Isabel might come through them, but she never did. At lunch-time I couldn't face the canteen stodge, so I bought a ham roll, and set off to eat it in lonely gloom in my chalet.

I walked out into the grounds, passing the girls' rooms on the way, and then it was that I spotted her through her ground-floor window. She was packing.

Should I go and say goodbye? No, better not.

The boys' chalets were just inside the lower end of the "short cut" my father had taken. I had gone a few yards up this track when a girl came out of the woods ahead of me. It was Isabel, dressed as I had seen her a few moments ago, in a cream suit with bracelets at her wrist and a gold locket at her neck. With the addition of a pair of black glasses.

She confronted me for a few moments. And then, trundling down the path from above, came a gardener with his wheelbarrow. For a moment I thought he was going to walk right through her; but she stepped across to the woods and disappeared among the trees.

It was perfectly clear that the gardener hadn't seen her at all.

I hesitated for a moment, then I turned tail and made for the Abbey as hard as I could run. I ran until I halted, panting, outside the girls' ground-floor windows again. And there, in her room, just as I had left her, was Isabel in her cream suit, without glasses, on her knees at her suitcase.

But now she was not packing, she was unpacking, as if at gunpoint.

I stared in at her, pressing my face to the glass. Presently she looked round and our eyes met, guiltily, as when you catch the glance of somebody in a mirror.

Then, with a violent start, she stared full at me, and she looked terrified. But why, why should she? I thought I had cause enough, but whatever was upsetting *her*?

3 What I did now doesn't show me in a very good light. My excuse is that I was bewildered and thoroughly scared, and also blindly angry that I should be so concerned with this wretched girl at all. I went to the end of the corridor where I knew she must eventually emerge and I waylaid her when she came up. She faltered when she saw me, and her cat-like face became so scared and hostile that I almost expected her to arch her back and hiss.

"Let me pass, please," she said, with a kind of old-fashioned snootiness; she might well have said, "Unhand me, sir." But she couldn't hide her fear, and this encouraged the bully in me.

"No," I said, "not till we've cleared something up. I want to know how you manage to be in two places at once."

She gave a little gasp, she looked pitiful, but I went on, brutally: "I want to know why you're playing hide-and-seek with me in the woods, why you made a late entry the other night and behaved like a bloody enchanted princess, and why you made me out a liar, and why you copied my drawing, because it was quite impossible for me to copy yours. Are you a conjuror or something? Magic and mystery? Because I don't want to be your straight man. Now, just what is your game?"

I felt ashamed of myself even while I was speaking, as if I were thumping her physically. All the haughtiness was knocked out of her, and now to my dismay, she began

19

crying. This softened me, of course. "Isabel," I said, "you haven't got a twin sister, have you?"

This idea had occurred to me before, although a twin sister who was visible to me alone was hard to explain. She wiped her tears as though furious with herself for shedding them, and said crossly, "No, I haven't." My weakening gave her strength. "I haven't got a twin sister, I don't know and don't care what you say you keep seeing, and I did *not*—"—this with a crushing charge of scorn—"I did *not* copy your drawing. Now will you please leave me alone."

So I left her alone, the brutal interrogator in me now in collapse. Although I was so plainly in the right, she had this flair for making me feel in the wrong. Was I having hallucinations? Ready to be led away by men in white coats? My boringly ordinary parents, that stolid gardener—they hadn't seen anything. Well, I had come down here in perfect health and as far as I knew I was about as psychic as a can of beans. Could you "catch" the habit of seeing things as you can flu? Having nothing else to do, I worried about myself. Leaving Isabel alone left me alone, too, because most of the students had paired off by now. I spent my time brooding and concocting all sort of fantasies. Fortunately the course kept me busy, but I had the evening and the night to get through, and I felt homesick, boring parents notwithstanding, and even thought of packing the course in.

To add to my misery, I was compulsively drawn to Isabel. It was absurd, but I was. To her of all people. By now I had found that not all the girls on the course were as high-and-mighty as I had thought them at first, and one of them might easily become the "nice girl friend" my mother was always wishing me to meet, but there was no help for it. Whenever I glanced at Isabel, my heart thumped. She looked furtively in my direction once or twice, but whenever our eyes met, she looked away.

On the afternoon of the following day, Jenny O'Brien took us on a coach trip to a museum near Ilminster, where there was an exhibition of West Country art. The other students were all chattering and laughing, and I envied them their carefree lives as I sat, downcast and smouldering, in the seat behind Isabel, longing to speak to her, but lacking the courage to start.

Jenny said, "Meet again at the coach at four-thirty, right?" and went into the museum with a little group of students. She tolerantly ignored the larger number who avoided the museum and went off into the wooded slopes behind it. I held back, nursing the wild hope that I might invite Isabel into those wooded slopes, but she, after also hanging back, went into the museum, so there was nothing for it but for me to slouch in myself.

I hung about, glowering at "Fishing Boats in the Harbour, Polperro", and so on, until I drifted through an archway into a smaller side room full of cases of stuffed birds, where there was no West Country art on show. There, sitting on a bench with her back to me, was Isabel. She did not hear me come in. Her hands were limp in her lap and her head was bowed. She said, very quietly and very intensely:

"Oh, *dear*."

It was heartbreaking. Well, to me it was. I could not stop myself; I went up to her and took her hands. "Isabel," I said, "can't you please tell me what's the matter?"

She said in a very small voice, "Did you really see something in the woods?"

I said mildly, "Sounds like something nasty in the woodshed! Isabel, I didn't see *something*, I saw you."

"Actually, you didn't, Michael."

"But—"

"You saw my double."

At which I went cold. But I strove to keep my voice light. I coaxed her: "Oh? And what does that mean?"

But instead of answering, she burst into a passionate fit of weeping: not the trickle of tears of the previous day, but a cascade; she was wracked with sobbing. She tried to speak, but her chin was quivering and the sobs kept engulfing the words, so that for all my concern she almost made me laugh.

"Oh, it's s-so aw-awful, I thought I'd g-got awa-ay from it and it's c-come ba-a-ack . . ."

"Don't cry," I kept repeating, helplessly. "Don't cry, don't cry . . ."

She quietened down. "I'm sorry I've been so rude."

"Well, I was tactless, I expect."

"No, you weren't. I owe you an explanation."

"Well, I must admit I'm curious."

"Not here, though."

"No, I can hear them coming. Look natural."

Jenny looked in, with her group of two or three students. They took quick stock of us, me self-conscious and Isabel red-eyed, murmured, "Oh, nothing in here," and discreetly withdrew.

"Bye-bye," said Isabel in their direction when they had gone, and actually smiled. "All right, Common Room after dinner?"

"All right," I said, my spirits wonderfully revived.

"Promise me something, though. *Don't* suggest I see a psychiatrist, will you?"

"You do know how to rouse one's curiosity," I said.

She stood up, walked a few paces with me, and then, to my great joy, put her arm round my waist and briefly hugged me.

"Are you enjoying this exhibition?"

"I'm going to from now on," I said, "but honestly, there's no one here as good as you are."

"Oh, I draw horrible things."

I fetched some coffee and sat down with her. The Common Room was part of what was called "The Mansion", and was rather luxurious, with armchairs you sank into. It was also nearly empty. The other students had discovered Newfield's night life—two pubs, in other words.

First of all she questioned me about the two times I had seen "her double", and how my parents and the gardener had not. She listened without once taking her gaze from my face, as though she were trying to learn my words by heart. She said: "It looks as if you and I are in this together, now."

"For better or worse," I said.

She didn't smile. "Mike, you're the only person who's ever seen her, apart from me."

"Well: who is she, Isabel?"

"I've got to begin at the beginning."

"All right."

"Well. When I was very small I had an imaginary friend. 'Imaginary' was my mother's word. I didn't know what it meant, but I liked using it, because it made me seem an interesting and important little girl. I'd tell my mother's visitors, 'I got a Majinry Friend', and they'd go into convulsions and coo at me, 'What's her name?' and I'd tell them: Libby. And they'd say, 'What's she like?' and I'd say, 'She's blind.'

"And then the visitor would stare at my mother and my mother would say, 'Yes, I don't know where she got that idea from! Certainly not from us!' and they'd go on discussing me as if I weren't there. My mother was rather proud of Libby's being blind. It marked me as a sensitive, caring child."

"Why did you imagine she was blind?" I asked curiously.

"I always thought of her as wearing black glasses.

"She was with me all the time. She went to bed with me and got up with me. Sometimes my mother imported other children to play with me—carefully selected, because she was a crashing snob—but I wasn't interested; Libby took up

23

all my attention. My mother was quite glad, really. 'Isabel's not like other children, she's highly artistic, a very imaginative child; she gets that from me, of course . . .' " Isabel gave an unladylike sniff.

"My mother liked to think that I was living in a sort of dream-paradise, like the fairyland gardens you read about in children's books, but it wasn't at all like that. Libby bossed me and bullied me and I was afraid of her. She made me do things."

"But she was imaginary?" I put in, frowning.

"No. 'Imaginary' was not my word and it was the wrong word. She was real."

"But what was she, a ghost?"

"No, no, not a ghost. Real."

"Could you see her?"

"No, not yet."

"I'm sorry," I said, "I'm getting lost—"

"Just listen, Mike.

"Sometimes their wills clashed. Libby's and my mother's. 'Come along, Isabel, time for bed.' 'Libby doesn't want me to go to bed.'

"It was true. Libby would be barring my way like a guard-dog. My mother would say, 'Oh, yes, Libby knows it's time little girls were in bed!' I knew she didn't know Libby and I would fly into a rage with her for being so stupid. And there'd be a session of kicking, screaming and rolling on the floor. I can't stick my mother," added Isabel, with calm detachment, "but I marvel at her patience. I wonder I didn't end up as a battered baby. All she did was keep saying, 'Whatever will Libby say? She won't want to play with little girls who make such a fuss!' And in the end Libby would tire of the game. She'd let me off, and there'd be no more war, and I'd be carried sobbing to bed."

"This sounds fairly normal, so far," I said.

"Yes, but it wasn't.

"My mother had a man friend called Malcolm, who was always calling on her, especially when my father was away. He was known to me as Uncle Malcolm, but he wasn't a real uncle. He was very kind to me, always bringing me presents. I hated him.

"I knew quite well that Malcolm had to win me round to please my mother, and so I made myself as vile as possible. I used to say, 'I don't want this horrible old present,' and my mother would be very vexed, but dear Malcolm always intervened and made excuses for me, all sympathy and fake kindliness.

"He bought presents for my mother, too. She collected china. That," said Isabel, with another sniff, "is the artistic bit. He was always turning up with Dresden shepherdesses and Coalport dishes. Well, he'd bought her a little pink and white cup and saucer—Minton, I think it was—and my mother put it on the glass shelf in the living room. One day when she'd left me alone for a few minutes, Libby got to work on me."

Isabel stopped.

"Go on," I prompted.

She gulped and sniffed again. "All right. In a minute."

After a pause she said, "Sorry. Well. Libby willed me to get that cup down and get myself a drink in it. And I did, I climbed on a chair and got the cup down, and went into the kitchen. I opened the fridge and got some orange juice and poured some into the cup and dragged a chair to the sink and climbed on it and filled the cup with water from the tap. All this Libby made me do. And just as I was going to drink, still standing on the chair, my mother came in.

"She cried out, and I panicked and tried to hide the cup from her, and I struck it against the tap and it smashed to bits.

"This time I was slapped and shaken and screamed at. 'Why did you do it? Oh, *why* did you do it?' And I

25

stammered, 'Libby . . .' And my mother looked horrible in her temper and she shouted, *'Don't you dare talk about Libby.* You know quite well there's no Libby. She's just an excuse for your horrid spiteful little ways.' And she shook me till my teeth rattled. *'Isn't she?'*

"And then a dreadful thing happened. My mother began crying as if she'd never stop. She said, 'You hate him, don't you? You hate him and you'd do anything to spite him. You're determined to spoil it all, aren't you?'

"We howled at each other on the kitchen floor. I tried to put my arms round her, but she pushed me away. I became so frantic that my sobbing turned to a kind of fit. At last she clutched me to her and knelt there staring over my head, and looking past her I saw Libby standing in the doorway."

"You saw her?" I said. "Clearly? As you can see me?"

"As clearly as I can see you."

"And what was she like?"

"She was exactly like me, except that she was wearing black glasses. And her expression. I was still crying."

"And she—?"

"Horrible glee."

"And after that you kept seeing her?"

"No, after that I didn't see her again. It was as if she'd achieved something and could give it a rest. For years after that she went out of my life."

Isabel found a tissue and dabbed at the tears that were trickling down her face.

"What happened to Malcolm?" I asked.

"Malcolm is now my stepfather. Yes, my mother's first marriage broke up. Malcolm has been a model stepfather. Terribly kind. Terribly understanding. Sent me to an expensive school. Took me to places. Bought me clothes. You know how much that green Liberty dress cost? Or the cream suit? Nothing too good for me. All to prove what a lovely man he was."

"Oh, dear," I said. "He just can't win, can he?"

"No, not with me.

"Anyway, Libby disappeared for years. And I should say that 'Libby' was just my baby-name for her. It was my way of saying her real name, Elizabeth. Does Elizabeth suggest anything to you?"

"It's another name for Isabel," I said.

"That's right. Isabel is the Spanish form of Elizabeth.

"I saw her again when I was nearly fourteen. The brink of adolescence, as they say. The psychiatrists have pounced on that. Actually, I felt her near me for quite some time before she appeared. I felt her presence. I turned dreamy and my schoolwork fell off. But my art work took an extraordinary new turn and I began drawing with power, with real power, and my art mistress got very excited and went running around saying that the school had produced a genius."

"She wasn't far wrong," I remarked.

"Thank you, Mike. Oh, it does matter to me, my drawing and painting. More than anything in the world. However.

"Malcolm had bought me a set of hairbrushes for my birthday, beautiful ones, and although I snubbed him when I took them, I really cherished them. In those days I wore my hair long. I was very vain about my hair. I'd go into my room and brush it and brush it and admire it in the mirror. One night, when I had brushed it forward over my shoulder, like a glossy black snake, I leaned forward to peer into its highlights, and then I saw that, whereas I was using one of Malcolm's brushes, the girl in the mirror was using a comb."

4 Isabel looked at me guardedly, as if expecting a laugh, but she certainly didn't get one.

"I went screaming downstairs and for a while I went all to pieces, and my parents called in the psychiatrists. You can imagine what a meal they made of it, because it was right out of a text-book: my parents' marriage was broken, I felt rejected, I was jealous of the second husband, I had compensated by inventing a child-companion, I'd developed hallucinations. All neatly worked out. But quite wrong. She was real, and she had come back."

"No one else ever saw her?"

"No."

"But you kept seeing her after that?"

"Yes, at first. I'd meet her on the stairs, or I'd wake in the night to find her at the foot of my bed, gazing at me."

"God."

"Well, it's amazing what you can get used to. I learned to live with her. She didn't seem to like being seen. She would always slink away as if she'd been caught red-handed in something. What I really dreaded was that someone else would see her."

"But surely, that would prove—"

"Ah, but don't you see, I didn't want proof. While I was the only one seeing her, I could kid myself that I really was hallucinating—though in fact I knew quite well that I wasn't. Anyway, no one saw her until you came along, and after a while I myself didn't see her any more; but I felt her near me all the time. She was always there. She was influencing my drawing. I was drawing much better, miles better. And do you know, I actually learned to use her influence against her, and drive her off."

"How?"

"By drawing, just by drawing. By drawing faces. She couldn't stand my doing that, it was her weak spot. There are supposed to be magic symbols that keep out evil spirits, aren't there? Well, my magic symbols were drawings. Drawings of faces. I lined my room with them. It was like building a wall round myself. I reckoned I'd beaten her, and my parents thought the psychiatrists had done the trick. No more foolish fancies. The highly-strung little neurotic was cured.

"So you can imagine how I felt, turning up here thinking all my past was behind me, only to have you chuck it at me again."

"Why should she appear to me?"

"I don't know. All I know is that I hated you. I thought you must be in league with her."

"But I—but I—"

"I know, Mike, I know, but I wasn't in a state to reason it out. I thought she'd found an ally. And then when you painted the grounds of our house—"

"What? That was the grounds of your house?"

She nodded, almost apologetically.

"How the hell did I do that?"

"I've changed my mind about you. I think you're being used."

"Used for *what*?" I demanded, so loudly that the only other occupant of the Common Room, deep in a book at the other end, looked round in alarm.

She shook her head hopelessly. "I think you may be in danger. I was wrong to hate you." Then, quaintly old-fashioned: "I think you're a good person."

Ever since I had heard her sigh, "Oh *dear*," in the museum, I had known that I was in love with her, but I could not find the words to tell her so.

At last I said: "I'm not her ally. I'm yours."

She was not consoled. "I didn't make you do the painting, did I?" she said.

Something extraordinary happened. I myself began drawing much better. I found out when we did a still life the next morning. I began drawing with passion. You wouldn't think much passion could go into a still life, consisting in this case of a brown tankard and a sort of ploughman's lunch, but it did. "Still" it might be, but it was alive with a life of its own.

The tutor passed me, made an encouraging remark, turned back as if suddenly struck, and went to the door.

"Jenny! Got a minute?"

Jenny O'Brien came in to see the phenomenon, and a small knot of students gathered round.

"Oh, yes," she said. "Not so much a still life, more a statement about the soul. Congratulations, Michael."

"Thank you," I said wanly.

"You look a bit fraught," she said curiously. "You're not still worrying about that other picture, are you?"

"I'm all right."

Jenny was still in the hall when our class ended, and as I came out, with Isabel at my side, she came up to me.

"Michael, I've never seen anyone look quite so distressed at being praised for a painting. Is anything worrying you?"

"That picture wasn't mine," I said.

At which Isabel turned pale, and Jenny looked impatient. "What?"

"It just wasn't mine. I just sat there and it flowed out of me. I painted it under influence."

"I know what you mean," whispered Isabel. "*She* was behind it."

"I suppose I should be grateful."

"Oh, no. She's not haunting you just to help you paint tankards nicely. That's just a side-effect."

Jenny listened to these asides grimly. "Would you please tell me what you are talking about?"

Isabel said, "It's impossible, Jenny," but I said, "Yes, we will. If you don't I will. I don't care what you say. We need to tell someone."

"Well!" said Jenny. "I'm sure you don't want me to die of curiosity. Shall we go?"

So we went to an empty classroom and told Jenny our tale. Some strange expressions crossed her face as she listened. She reminded me of a priest who is obliged to hear a confession of a crime.

"Interesting to know how she managed to make herself a pair of black glasses," she remarked at last. "We'd be on our way to learning the secret of creation."

"That would be a great help," said Isabel.

Jenny addressed herself to me. "You've seen this double twice. The first time your parents didn't see her, and the second time the gardener didn't. So you've got no witnesses. Doesn't that suggest that the experience was entirely subjective?"

"But, Jenny," I exclaimed, "I came down here all innocent and I saw this girl in the woods. Why should I have got subjective all of a sudden? Subjective about what?"

"So you're going to insist that what you saw had a supernatural cause?"

"Yes, I am. I'm forced to."

Jenny's face darkened. "If I were you, I should be very, very careful before you attribute anything to the supernatural. I should leave it as a last resort, and even then reject it. I grew up in a village in County Mayo where the folk were absolutely pixilated by superstition. Everyone believed in bogles and banshees and the Little People, and tales were told in every bar of things they'd Seen with Their Very Eyes. I learned very early in life that where the supernatural is concerned, you can't separate the truth from wishful thinking and plain lying."

Isabel stood up. "Miss O'Brien," she said, "I didn't grow up in an Irish village, I don't know what a bogle is, I'm not pixilated, I assure you that I'm not thinking wishfully, and you must take my word for it that I'm not lying. So your bit of autobiography isn't much use to me. But thank you for listening."

Jenny's face relaxed. "Sit down, sit down, girl," she said. "I'm sorry, I didn't mean to upset you. I fly off the handle when the supernatural is mentioned. I heard so much about it, not only in the village, but in my own family. My grandmother was supposed to be a witch. In point of fact, she was a gruesome old thing who would tell you anything for a glass of gin. I was a sceptical child and I grew sick of the tales they told about her. She was clairvoyant, and knew when people were going to die."

"How?" I asked.

"This will interest you. She saw apparitions of them."

"Apparitions of living people?"

"So she said."

"Well, that's amazing."

"I saw an apparition of *myself*," murmured Isabel gloomily.

But Jenny was not listening to her. "What's really amazing is that people believed her. Just listen to this. She was supposed to have seen a spirit-image of my own mother, aged seven. There was a fire at the village school, and Mother was very frightened, and she appeared to my grandmother in the kitchen, a little ghost-girl, crying 'Mummy!' And Grandma knew all about the fire long before any of the neighbours. Now, what's wrong with that tale?

"Well, you'd know if you knew our village. It was a tiny

little place and a fire in the school would have been spotted immediately by everybody, so Grandma couldn't have had private knowledge of it. Never mind. The tale was told to every visitor. They wanted to believe it. The truth didn't interest them."

"All the same, you haven't proved that she didn't see something," I said.

"No, Michael, but no one can prove that she did. We only had her word for it."

Work filled up the afternoon for us, but we spent the whole evening discussing what Jenny had said; or rather, I spent it trying to soothe Isabel, who was smouldering with resentment and despair. For myself, Jenny's strong personality had had an effect on me. In spite of everything, I began struggling again with the possibilities of hallucination, auto-suggestion and the like, but, discreetly, I didn't tell Isabel about my doubts.

It was late when I finally went back to my room, with none of the boys to keep me company. The night was cloudy and dark, with the moon never quite breaking the clouds, and under the trees it was pitch black.

As I turned into the "short cut" I grew afraid of the dark like a child. It was as if my nerves were having revenge on me for my doubts. I felt that someone else was walking beside me. The feeling grew till I had to force myself to put the next foot forward. It was here that I had twice seen Isabel's double. Two or three times I whirled round, and once I even called out, "Who's there?" in a shaky voice. When nothing answered, I became sure that something was waiting for me, in my chalet.

When I reached my door I was trembling. I opened it and switched on the light.

Oh, God! A figure stood before me! A tall, thin, white-faced form, staring into my face!

Well, now you can see the state I was in. There was a three-quarter-length mirror on the wall beside the washbasin, and I was looking at my own reflection. Ridiculous, isn't it? I sat on the edge of my bed and held my head for shame.

The force of all we had said about the power of the imagination came home to me. My own thoughts had got me into this state. I had nearly passed out when I had looked at that mirror.

It took me a good ten minutes to pull myself together. Calmed down at last, and disgusted with myself, I went to the door and opened it to get some fresh air. The light from my chalet poured on to the trees. And into that patch of light came the figure of Elizabeth, barefoot and wearing a white nightdress such as I suppose Isabel herself was wearing at the time. The light caught her black glasses as she turned to me. They flashed for a moment like silver pools.

She waited for several seconds, her opaque shining glasses directed at me, and then she turned, walked down the path a few steps, and then off into the woods again to be lost in shadows. She did not exactly vanish. She receded and was swallowed up. I closed the door and sat on the edge of my bed.

I had seen her much more definitively this third time. She was solid, not a transparent ghost, and yet quite silent, and she moved, apparently, without effort. She was exactly like Isabel and yet different. The cat qualities were emphasized. She seemed powerfully feline. Her face, caught in the light, was a livid white. I guessed why she wore black glasses. It was not because she was blind, but because her eyes were too terrible to see.

5 My chalet was one of about a dozen, but I felt like Crusoe marooned on his island, with a sinister and possibly cannibalistic Girl Friday lurking outside. I did not dare venture out, nor go to bed either, for fear of being off guard; and besides, I was afraid I might dream.

But then, to solve this problem, I was overcome with drowsiness so heavy and sudden that I hardly had time to get out of my clothes, and I slept deeply till morning.

I did not know how to tell Isabel, who presumably had slept through it all. This relationship of ours was a heavy responsibility. For obvious reasons I was her first boy friend, and a unique one: a genuine "soul-mate", you might say. I had often had romantic visions of being someone's soul-mate, but there is a debit side to everything, and there were elements in this that I certainly hadn't bargained for.

All through the first part of the morning I was morose and silent. Isabel, you may be sure, noticed it.

"Mike, what are you thinking about?"

"Nothing."

"You must be thinking about something."

"Nothing important."

"If it's that unimportant why can't you tell me?"

And so on. It was restrictive to have a girl friend. There was no freedom, even to think. It was also rather depressing. All supernatural considerations apart, ever since I had fallen in love a slight melancholy had hung over me, a background insistence like the hum from a tube of strip-lighting. This now became tinged with irritation.

"I've told you. It's nothing."

"Oh, dear. A regular little ray of sunshine, aren't you?"

"Oh, shut up."

It was the coffee-break, and we were jammed side by side on two chairs against the wall. Isabel did not take offence. She contemplated me.

"What's the next lecture?"

"Science of Perspective."

"Stuff Science of Perspective. Come on."

She took my hand, pulled me from the room, and hurried me from the college. We went through all that little scene unnoticed; the students were jammed so close that we slipped out under cover. Running most of the way, we made for a café opposite the Abbey, where they sold dainty teas at exorbitant prices.

"You've seen her again, haven't you?"

"Yes."

"I could tell. What happened?"

Telling her brought on a fit of shuddering, and Isabel reached across the table to steady my hands. Her face was full of dread. "I'd sooner you'd seen a ghost," she said. "Ghosts make more sense."

"Yes. Isabel, *what* is she?"

"Well, the psychiatrists said she was created out of my own mind, you know, by persecution complexes and neurotic fears and all that. You don't believe that, do you?"

"No."

"No. The neurotic fears were created by *her*, more like it. But the shrinks would never allow that. Well, all except one."

"And who was he?"

"A German. Dr Diener. I liked him. He was very patient with me. Mind you, I could never be certain that he wasn't just humouring me. They all humoured me," added Isabel with fury, "as if I were a lunatic—"

"But what did he say, this Dr—um—?"

"Diener. Oh, you could never pin him down. He said things like 'man knows very little as yet about the nature of the spirit', and he said that we couldn't be certain that all the old superstitions were wrong."

"Like, more things in heaven and earth . . .?"

"Yes, right."

"He sounds the best of the bunch."

"Yes, he was, and so, sure enough, my folks stopped sending me to him. They said he was encouraging me in my delusions. Or something of the sort."

"But I'm not deluded," I exclaimed. "If I got in touch with him and told him—"

"You'd have a job. He was very offended at being taken off the case. And Mike, he costs the earth."

I brooded for a few moments. "Why ever should she appear to me?" I muttered at last.

"I don't know, Mike. It's terrible to have to keep on, keep on saying that, but I just don't know." Isabel shook her head, frowning. "There's something about the atmosphere of this place that helps her. Maybe the artistic set-up. Or maybe not. I just don't know. She seems sensitive to paintings and drawings, for some reason—"

"You said something about your drawings keeping her away?"

"Yes, there are some drawings that she hates. And once again, I don't know why."

"Could I draw them?"

"Yes, I think you could, but she'll fight you with your own weapons. She'll make you draw what she wants if she can. But you can use it against her. It isn't easy. You can't just draw any old thing. You've got to think something up that will really check her and you've got to believe in it while you're working, really believe in it."

"God," I said. My own upbringing hadn't conditioned me to this sort of thing. "Right in Magic Spell country, isn't it?"

"Yes, so is she."

"But it'll work?"

"She'll interfere if she can."

At the end of the second week, halfway through the course, the college was holding a "Prelim. Exhibition" of students' work, open to the public. Elizabeth, meanwhile, made no further move. Isabel, however, kept a close eye on me. (Yes, rather than the other way round!) Our relationship by now did not seem to have lasted mere days, or even years; it was a stable fact of our existence, as if we were brother and sister. Isabel had become affectionately bossy. Although always ready to duck, so to speak, if I lost my temper, she had a sort of magic hold on me simply by being a girl; and I can't say I minded.

I wasn't going to tell my parents about the exhibition, but Isabel insisted.

"Write and tell your mother. If you don't, she'll go mad."

"How do you know?"

"I just do."

She was so right that I marvelled that I hadn't realized it myself. Yes, wasn't my mother always upset when I failed to tell her about school plays, Open Days, and the like, and wasn't I always in the doghouse for it? Couldn't I already hear her injured tones again? So I did write, giving my mother a pen-picture of most of the exhibits, and rather gushingly hoping that she and Dad would be able to make it.

Actually, I hoped the opposite. I imagined my mother looking Isabel over and sizing her up, all so discreetly that

38

Isabel would guess at once what she was up to; and I imagined my father nudging Isabel and saying, "Here, don't let him start drawing *you* in the Altogether, will you?" which would humiliate and degrade me; and if that shows me to be a snob, too bad.

So I was relieved to get a letter from my mother turning the visit down. "It all sounds *so* interesting from your description, I'm sure you know we'd love to come—Dad will only just have got back from Newcastle next Friday and he'd be tired—it's a long drive to Newfield—we think it would be better if we came at the *end* of the course—two weeks next Friday—we're both so glad you're enjoying it so much and it will do you good to be in contact with *'fellow artists'*!!!—is *Isabel* very good at drawing? . . ." My mother's English always was a bit shaky, but it was a nice letter.

"Yes, very nice," said Isabel. "You don't deserve her. You don't know how lucky you are."

"Is your mother coming?"

"I expect she'll show up, but she can stay at home for all I care."

"Now who's talking?"

"I don't want to see her."

'You've really got it in for her, haven't you? But she's looked after you. She must have some feelings for you."

"Oh, she has. She hates me."

There was no talking her out of this mood.

"I did love her terribly when I was little, but she's not my mother any more, she's Malcolm's wife, and he can have her . . . . Well, I thought I loved her when I was little, but that psychiatrist, Dr Diener, he threw up a few things. Delved into my infancy, you know. He made me remember lying in my cot and crying while my mother and father brought the house down quarrelling . . . Banging and shouting and screaming . . . And there'd be awful silences, which frightened me all the more, because I supposed one of them was dead . . . I don't know what good Dr Diener thought he was doing. I liked him, though."

We were being allowed to show three pictures each in the exhibition. Isabel had no problem. I had seen her portfolio by now. She drew everything well, but mainly she drew faces. They were marvellous, but very disturbing. They were tormented, as if they were full of dismay from the shock of being born. Their eyes seemed to follow you and accuse you with their stare, as though you had no right to happiness. They had come from some dark mature place in Isabel's mind, much older than her daily self.

"Are they real people?" I asked.

"No, I imagined them. They're states of mind."

"Very worried states of mind!"

"Yes, but they just came naturally. I didn't feel suicidal or anything when I did them."

"And are these the 'magic symbols' that keep her away?"

"That's right."

"What made you think of doing them?"

"Impossible to say. They've worked."

"Until I came along. I wish I could learn the trick of it."

"One thing I must never do," said Isabel, "is a self-portrait. There's one image too many of me already."

"What about other people drawing you?"

"No way. I won't be photographed either."

"Oh, dear."

I had been longing to draw her myself. I had one good picture for the exhibition, the still life, but otherwise I felt that the pictures I had drawn weren't nearly so good as the ones I was going to draw.

"My picture of you was going to overtake the Mona Lisa in the charts."

"I'm sorry, Mike, but it's not on."

"I know what I'll do," I said. "I'll ask Jenny if I can draw her."

40

"Yes, why don't you?" said Isabel, but with distinct coldness.

"She'd make a good subject."

"Perfect. No doubt you'll put your heart into it."

I really am very lacking in foresight. It was stupid of me to suggest this to Isabel. "I'll do my best," I said.

"She's sweet on you, you know."

"Rubbish."

"Don't you think she's attractive?"

"She's all right."

"With those green eyes? She's fabulous."

"Anyway, she's old enough to be my—"

"Sister?"

"Isabel, what is this?"

"Oh, I'm not saying she's madly in love with you, but there is some sort of attraction. Can't you see that?"

"No. Is this another of your intuitions? I'm not with it this time."

"No, Mike," said Isabel sadly, "I know you're not."

I hadn't told Jenny of Elizabeth's last visitation, even though it proved my tale. I was squeamish about subjecting it to the light of her disbelief. I liked Jenny, and wanted her to respect me.

I approached her diffidently about the portrait, because after all she was a tutor and I was only a student, but she was pleased.

"I shall add it to my collection."

"Have a lot of students drawn you, then?"

"Thousands. Why isn't Isabel being given this honour?"

"She won't let anyone draw her."

"Ah. She's afraid Alice might come through the looking-glass after her, is she? Oh dear oh dear, she is superstitious, isn't she?"

"You know what I have to say about that, Jenny."

"Yes," said Jenny, with a sigh. "I wish I could talk you out of it. I hate to say it, but she's not very good for you in some ways."

"You don't like her much, do you?"

"I think very highly of her talent," said Jenny judicially. "There's no questioning that. She may be a bit too self-absorbed, that's all. As I've said, she tends to dramatize herself. I mean, why send me that heroic letter, when she obviously intended to stay on anyway?"

"She couldn't help herself. She was compelled to stay on."

"There's no dissuading you, is there?"

"Why are you so concerned about me, Jenny? In an art college you must meet plenty of nut-cases."

"The frame of mind you're in can do you harm," she said soberly. It was not a satisfactory answer, but I dropped the matter.

She sat at the lecturer's table, resting her arms on it, and I began making the rough sketches for a head-and-shoulders likeness. Studying her like this, I saw that Isabel was right about Jenny's looks. She had a beautiful, strong face, with the rather high cheek-bones and the wide mouth of her race, and her near-black hair, and her marvellous green eyes. An intelligent, thoughtful face. A good subject.

But all the same, I couldn't get it right. I scribbled and frowned and rubbed out; I discarded that piece of paper and started another; and another. I began to feel uneasy.

"Having trouble, Michael? Don't you like what you see?"

I scowled and sketched a bit more, without answering.

"Sorry. I'll keep quiet."

Not long after this Jenny began to look ill. I should have asked her how she felt, but I was too worried about my sketches. They were not coming out right at all. I dropped one after the other on the floor at my feet.

You see, I was not drawing Jenny at all. Every time I put pencil to paper I was drawing Isabel.

42

I was very conscious of what Jenny had just said about giving in to foolish superstition, and all that; but now I could swear that my hand was being moved. I was just not in control of this. I was being used.

I was now fighting a rising panic. I don't know what I would have done next, but Jenny put a stop to it. She put her head down on her arms and groaned.

"Michael, I'm sorry, I can't go on."

I hurried to her. "What is it, Jenny?"

"Migraine."

"Can I get you an aspirin or something?"

"No, I must lie down. I get these from time to time. I never know why."

Her eyes were dark with pain. She groped her way from the room. I gathered up my extraordinary sketches and tore them into minute pieces. As I did so I was filled with mortal fear of doing something fatal. But my reason told me not to be ridiculous. What possible harm could tearing paper do?

6 No one was harmed, it seemed, except myself. It had upset me to tear those sketches. I felt guilty, for no good reason. My mind kept dwelling on how Isabel must have felt, aged three, when she broke the cup.

I never did get round to drawing Jenny again. My first attempt had discouraged me. Perhaps Jenny felt the same.

"I hope she's all right," I said.

"So you have said about sixteen times already," said Isabel.

"Oh, have I?"

"You have a tendency to repeat yourself."

"Oh."

Jenny took a day's rest from lectures and then returned looking normal. "Sorry about that," she said. "Migraine. I wouldn't wish it on anyone."

"It wasn't my fault, was it?"

"No, no. I've had them since I was a child. Not very often, fortunately."

"Do they know what causes them?"

"No, they're a mystery."

There were too many mysteries, I reflected. Science was clueless about a lot of things.

Meanwhile there were no more signs from Elizabeth, unless you counted my fretful wish to draw Isabel, which of course I couldn't carry out. This grew quite morbid. If you yourself paint or write poetry perhaps, you'll know how it feels to want to produce something and be frustrated; your mind sulks like the air before a thunderstorm. I remembered Jenny's warning not to see psychic significance in everything, and told myself that my feelings were normal, but I did not convince myself, nor did I believe that Elizabeth had really relaxed her vigil. This quiet was like the lull of gunfire on a battlefield.

The day of the exhibition arrived. The visitors began flowing in, with a few parents and local pressmen among them; and there was even a crocodile of thirteen-year-olds from the local school, who began taking notes, poor kids, under the eye of a very earnest-looking woman teacher. We sat by our exhibits like salesmen, or strolled with the crowd, looking for the twentieth time at one another's work.

After about half an hour, Isabel's mother and stepfather arrived. I marvelled, looking at this middle-aged pair, that they could ever have gone through all the hoo-ha of an illicit love affair. Grand passions at best end up in tedium, I suppose. Isabel's stepfather was pudgy, bespectacled, and politely smiling; he trailed round after his wife, always a deferential step behind. He had made a lot of money in his time, I understood, and must have had a good head for business, but perhaps he had burned up all his personality getting there, because, for all I saw of him that day, he was such a lay figure in the life of his family that he might as well have been stuffed. His name, by the way, was Harper. Isabel retained the name of her real father.

Mrs Harper was very like Isabel; but a crystallized version, as it were. Where Isabel's cat-like properties were deliciously lissom, her mother's were stringy. Her eyes were also dark-brown, but beady. She looked alert and watchful and faintly disdainful, as though she were aware that nothing could quite reach her own standards. Her hair was greying, and she was most expensively dressed.

Isabel's stand and mine were separated by the whole width of the room, because the exhibits had been arranged in alphabetical order. Her parents went to her first, of course,

45

but I knew that I was under scrutiny from the moment her mother had seen the name on my stand. And sure enough, after a while Mrs Harper drifted over to me, leaving her husband to engage Isabel. She shook hands with me, and said:

"It's Michael, isn't it? We've heard so much about you!"

Now the truth was, she had heard, or read, one sentence about me. I had seen the picture letter-card which Isabel had reluctantly written home, and I was sure this was the only communication her parents had received. Isabel was not a good letter-writer. The sentence was, "There's a boy here called Michael Wilkinson who draws very well and we have looked at each other's work." At the end of the note Isabel had put: "I thought I was going to hate it here, but I think I'm going to enjoy it after all."

But, where their children's affairs are concerned, mothers are telepathic. I myself had said in my letter home, "I've met a girl named Isabel Carrick." When Mother had written back, "Is *Isabel* good at drawing?" that underlining of "Isabel" was absolutely loaded with significance. Mothers catch on like lightning. Mrs Harper had decided that I mattered.

She was quivering with eagerness to question me. But conditions were difficult; the room was crowded, and visitors occasionally looked at my work and questioned me on it, so that she was obliged to keep up a pretence of holding an agreeable discourse with me, her voice pleasant and her lips fixed in a smile, while her narrow dark eyes searched frantically for an opening. Moreover, Isabel, on the other side of the room, was showing signs of the most acute impatience to come over and listen to what we were saying.

Her stepfather would not have been able to hold her back any longer, but, as luck would have it, the Principal of the college strolled up at that moment and began holding the two of them in chat. Mrs Harper, glancing across, saw that she had only a minute's grace. I must say for her, she went straight to the point.

She said hurriedly: "Listen, Michael. I want to talk to you about Isabel. It's impossible to talk here. Will you come and see us? By yourself?"

"I—"

"Tomorrow. We can pick you up just outside the college. We can't manage tonight because we're taking Isabel out to dinner. Tomorrow. Say, seven o'clock?"

"I—"

"Make some excuse to get away. You do appreciate that you must come alone, don't you?"

"Well, I—"

"*Please.*"

It was a conspiracy, and I was a terribly inexperienced conspirator. Besides, this woman had no idea of Isabel's real trouble. She related everything to herself. But then I, too, was desperate to do anything that would help Isabel, and also, God knows, help myself.

"She's coming across. *Please.*"

"Yes, all right."

"Hallo, darling," said Mrs Harper as Isabel came up. "Michael and I have been having such an interesting chat. He's been telling me all about his work."

"Has he? I don't suppose you understood a word of it," said Isabel.

"Sorry you were subjected to that," said Isabel.

"Look," I said severely, "normally you are a passable human specimen, but you weren't just then. You were awful."

"I know," said Isabel meekly. "She makes me sick, that's all."

"Did you have to be so rude?"

"She makes me. Sorry. You can smack me if you like."

"Don't be ridiculous, and behave yourself."

"All right. Michael, has she invited you to come to dinner with us tonight?"

"Er—no," I said, with a slight start.

"Oh. Well, if she does, could you please say no? I can't sit through dinner while she cross-examines you. Because that would be the object."

"Oh, yes, sure, if she does."

"What will you do tonight?"

"Go down to the pub with some of the crowd, I expect."

"I'm so worried about you," said Isabel, "going back to that chalet."

"It preys on my mind a bit, too," I said, "but what can I do about it? People carry crucifixes to ward off vampires, don't they? Pity she's not just a simple-minded vampire."

"I tell you what. You can have a couple of my pictures of faces to put up in your chalet. They do work against her. They can be your crucifixes."

"She's not come into the chalet yet, she stops me on the way. Perhaps I'd better wear them like sandwich boards."

"Mike," said Isabel, "I think you're terrific."

"Oh, do you? Why?"

"It's so brave of you to make a joke of it."

I was not joking because I was brave; I was joking because I was frightened. Joking is often our excuse for saying things we dare not say seriously. Jokes are meant.

Isabel found me two of her drawings, brilliant studies of women with gaunt and stricken faces, and I fixed them up in my defence, one on the inside of my chalet door, and one fastened with safety pins on the inside of my anorak. I was glad Jenny couldn't see me, for I'm sure her scorn would have withered me. But if ever you've touched wood or thrown salt over your shoulder, you'll sympathize, I hope.

Isabel's parents took her out to lunch, and made periodic appearances at the exhibition throughout the afternoon, because unlike the other visitors they were staying in Newfield all day. In between times, I understood, they hobnobbed with the Principal. Mr Harper had given a donation to the college. "He would," said Isabel. "He paves his way to popularity with money. He thinks he can buy everything."

They took her out to dinner in the evening, too, without, of course, inviting me, and I went to the pub and played gooseberry to two couples until closing time, buying drinks for them lavishly but rationing myself to a very limited quantity of shandy. My object was to ensure some company on the way back to the chalets, because I dreaded that walk along the path through the woods. I foresaw difficulty, because neither couple would want me hanging around, but fortunately one boy did go back briefly to his chalet before setting out again, and I trekked along with him and gained the inside of my room. I mention all this to show the fugitive life I was leading. Nerves. They were working me like a puppet.

I hung my anorak, after consideration, over the window, and went to bed. In spite of my worries, I had been sleeping very well at Newfield, even more heavily than usual, but I never put my head on the pillow without fear of dreaming. I can't exactly explain why. I dreaded that Elizabeth, which was too fine a name for that prowling thing who could invade your thoughts, would get inside my mind while it was at large in dream and possess it with some monster of her own. This night I did dream, a horrible dream, although she had no part in it. I was in an enormous room, dark and cavernous. A little child was running frantically about. Sometimes the child was myself, sometimes Isabel, sometimes without identity; what was constant was its blind terror, because in a corner two grown-ups lay dead, and it could not make anyone hear. Sometimes the grown-ups were my parents, sometimes Isabel's, sometimes no one I knew. Outside an unearthly din was raging: thunder and rain, a howling of cats, and the yelling of a mob, whose ugly menacing words were smothered in the uproar. The child sobbed and panted, dashed and zig-zagged and collided. No one came.

7 I didn't actually lick my lips furtively, but I felt like doing so, when I told Isabel: "I shan't be in tonight. Got to go out."

"Oh? Where?"

"Erm—going to see an aunt."

"An *aunt*?" repeated Isabel, as though of all relatives this was the least conceivable. "Where does she live, your aunt?"

"Somerset."

"Well, that's precise, I must say. Well, I'd like to meet her. Are you going to take me?"

"I can't, really. You see—"

"Oh, all right, I know when I'm not wanted."

"Oh, no, it's not like that—"

"I don't believe you're going to see an aunt at all."

"Oh, yes—"

"I think your aunt lives in Wiltshire, not Somerset, in a house called 'Wildfell Lodge'. You've already painted the front garden. You can't miss it."

I was no match for her. I felt like some inept baddy whose guns had been shot out of his hands by Wyatt Earp.

"I knew it. I knew she'd get at you," said Isabel, who was much less put out than I had expected. "I knew she was simply writhing with curiosity about you. But don't feel flattered. You'll just be helping her with her enquiries, like they do the police. She'll pump you about me. She doesn't talk to many people, you see. That's one of the penalties of being a snob. She keeps on at Malcolm, but she might as well talk to the cat as talk to him. I think it was a bit feeble of you to agree."

"Well, it's to help myself. Your double has transferred herself to me down here, and I want to get all the help I can."

"What help do you expect?"

"I suppose, bits of information that might put me in the picture."

"A fat lot of help you'll get from her."

The Rolls-Royce met me at the top of the drive. Throughout the journey, Malcolm strained for things to say: was I enjoying the course? And what was I on just now? That must be very interesting. I, too, strained with uninspired politeness to answer him, while all the time I was getting more and more worked up inside at the prospect of seeing the house and grounds which I had seen already with my mind's eye.

The Harpers lived just over the border of Wiltshire. The car left the main road and went off down a labyrinth of by-lanes into what seemed to be an estate, of such poshness that the houses were as far apart as buildings in a safari park.

We reached Wildfell Lodge. Yes, I had been here before, as it were. It was the strangest feeling. The place was more familiar, in a way, than my own house or school, because I'd never really paid attention to them, whereas this I had somehow observed and reproduced. My painting had been far from photographic, but I had got all the features right: the trees, the shrubs, the climbing roses trailing between posts on long loops of ropes, and the ornamental lake; and above all, the iron railings, black with gilded tops; they were so vivid they seemed to spring up out of the ground at me. I recognized the white house, far back.

The August evening was still light, but the sky was overcast, and Malcolm switched on his lights as he entered the grounds. They made shadows lunge and rear as we passed the trees, and when they swept the lake they made it flash like the black glasses of Elizabeth. I half expected to see her standing in the shadows, waiting for me. I felt as though I were about to enter a haunted house, not a modern home.

Inside, it was more like a museum than a home. You never saw so much elegant junk. Mrs Harper must have been collecting non-stop since Isabel broke that cup. China, silver, old furniture, pictures. Terribly good taste. I couldn't fit Isabel into it at all. You'd have had to petrify her and stand her in some corner, like a statue.

Her mother was no statue. She was all a-twitch, not with vitality, but fretfully, as if she couldn't understand why she was so discontented. All through dinner she questioned me. Where did I live? Redhill? Ah, that was a very good residential area, wasn't it? How large was my house? What school did I go to? What was my father's job?—An Advertising Executive; that must be stimulating work. Perhaps I had my talent from him?

In all, I think, Mrs Harper decided that I was quite a relief. Not all that could be desired, perhaps, but not as bad as she'd feared.

She lowered her voice. "Well, I'm glad Isabel has met . . ."—she hesitated—". . . someone to share her interests. She has not had an easy time of it, and she finds making friends very difficult. Did you know that she had a nervous breakdown two years ago?"

I'd heard about it, I said.

"She actually started having hallucinations, you know. Or perhaps you don't."

Yes, I did know.

"Indeed? You seem to have won her confidence. It's more than I can say. I've tried my best, but she just clams up and becomes extremely rude. Goodness knows, we've been to enough trouble. We've paid out a small fortune in psychiatrists' fees . . ." Mrs Harper checked herself for a moment, clearly afraid that she'd said too much, but there was one thing she was burning to ask:

"What has she told you about me?"

I took the bull by the horns.

"She says that when she was about three years old you smacked her for breaking a cup."

"*That*'s what she remembers!" She turned to her husband, who was attending with an expressionless face. "Isn't that typical! The only time I ever laid a hand on her, and she chooses to remember that! Not the countless times we've strained our patience trying to understand her, indulging her whims . . . Do you know, there was a time when she became hysterical if she saw anyone wearing dark glasses . . . Ah! you find that odd, do you? And then, refusing to be photographed. Another of her little foibles. One would like a record of one's only child, naturally, but this has always been an obsession with her. Our last photo of her is of when she was three!" Mrs Harper fished a photograph album from under the coffee-table and opened it. "You see?"

The photo showed a diminutive child in red dungarees, looking gravely at the camera. I realized that I was looking not only at Isabel, but at Libby, as Isabel had seen her once. I could not take my eyes from it.

"You seem really taken with it, Michael!" said Mrs Harper. She gave me a kind smile, unlike her usual artificial one. "Would you like to have it? We have a copy."

As she handed it to me she said, quite quietly, "Everything I've said will get back to her, won't it? And I shall be a bigger villain than ever . . . You know that I married twice, don't you?"

"Yes."

"Yes. Well, what of it? How many marriages end in divorce these days? One in three, isn't it? Do all children

53

behave like Isabel? I think the psychiatrists indulged her too much, personally. There was one in particular, a German—"

"Dr Diener," I said.

"Oh, you are well-informed. Yes, Dr Diener. He encouraged her quite absurdly. You'd have thought he was trying to make her worse."

Her husband spoke for the first time. "There's a bit about him in the paper," he said, "if I can find it—"

"Oh, never mind now, Malcolm," said his wife impatiently.

I felt sorry for him. Having come through smoke and flame to achieve this marriage, he found himself on a siding, for his wife was concerned with nothing but Isabel. I did not like Mrs Harper. All the same, it is not only people who wear haloes who have strong feelings. Whatever Isabel might say, it was clear that her mother thought about her non-stop.

I turned to Malcolm. "Please, I'd like to see it," I said.

He fetched the paper. I read:

"Dr Hans Diener, consultant psychiatrist to leading London hospitals and author of several books on psychology, has for the past ten years been working at a book entitled *Art and Magic*, a subject in which he has a profound interest.

"The earliest artists, the cave-dwellers, says Dr Diener, did not think of themselves as artists at all, but as magicians. They painted animals in order to have power over them, making them easier to catch when they hunted them. He finds that the thread of this belief runs through all the ages. Modern man may be wrong in supposing that he has risen above it.

"His publishers declare that this is the most important work on symbolic magic since Sir James Frazer's *The Golden Bough*.

"It is now completed, except for some appendixes, in which Dr Diener intends to examine case histories of people who have had supernatural experiences connected with art.

54

Anyone who has had such an experience, or who knows of one, involving magic charms, designs, tokens, and the like, is invited to write to . . ."

I handed the paper to Mrs Harper. She skimmed the piece briefly.

"Good heavens, in this day and age," she remarked. "Drawing things to ward off devils. How much is he getting paid for that, I wonder?"

We talked on and on. I got nothing from it, for all that I could see, and Mrs Harper got the relief of talking. She watched me closely all the time.

"Come and see us again," she said, when I left.

As I waited for a moment in the hall I heard her whisper to her husband:

"Oh, yes, he's dotty about her. You can see that."

It was raining, and Malcolm drove me right to the door of my chalet, using my father's "short cut". It happened that I was wearing a suit, which my mother had forced me to pack in spite of my protests, in case some social event should occur which required one. I hadn't transferred Isabel's drawing to the jacket—it hung open and would have looked ridiculous —and I felt like a gangster who has left off his bullet-proof waistcoat as we went through this sensitive area. But lights were on in the neighbouring chalets and there was a feeling of life about the place, and no black-spectacled figure glided out of the trees to confront me.

It was late, the students were turning in, and I decided not to seek out Isabel till the morning. I went to bed, and lay thinking about the Harpers and their wealth, and the emptiness of their lives, and wondered whether it *had* to be like this. I mean, were there only two choices, to feel deprived when you hadn't got it, or cheated when you had?

When the lights were out, and all was still, I heard a rustling at my bedside cabinet, right by my head. I thought

55

of rats, and not with much relief either, because the thought of one scrabbling away close to my ear was not pleasant. But it might be the wind; the chalet was draughty. Then the rustling stopped. I remembered how silly I'd been about my own reflection and I resolved not to make a monster out of nothing again.

Then something rolled the length of my cabinet-top and fell on to the floor. My ball-point pen.

And I remembered that I had wedged that pen behind my folder of notes on the cabinet, and it couldn't have rolled off, unless it had been moved.

I pulled the clothes over my head and lay huddled under them for a long time; then with a sudden spasm I jumped out of bed, switched on the light, picked up my pen from the floor, and examined my folder of notes.

It was open, although I had certainly put it there closed. It was open at the last page I had written on, two or three lines of notes on Jenny's last History of Art lecture.

Underneath my notes was written, in deeply-scored block capitals, as if the pen had been clutched in a fist:

MICHAEL
DRAW ME

8 "Well?" demanded Isabel the next morning.

I began cautiously. "I heard your mother say that anyone can see I'm dotty about you."

"Anyone but Malcolm, she means. He wouldn't see the bloody arrows on St Sebastian. *Are* you?"

"Oh, yes," I said apathetically.

"You look awful," said Isabel, with sudden alarm. "What's wrong?"

Reluctantly I showed her the thick black capitals in my notes. I had even wondered whether, being a kind of spirit-writing, they would disappear, but they hadn't, and their marks were scored on the page underneath.

"Oh, *Mike*! How did—when did this happen?"

"In the middle of the night."

"You're—you're sure you didn't do it yourself?"

I had thought of this myself—a sleepwalker's action—but all the same I snapped at her.

"Quite sure. Did you?"

"Oh, Mike! Did I pick the lock, or get in through the ventilator?"

"I know, I know. Actually I heard it happen."

"I'm never going to let you out of my sight," said Isabel, a trifle hysterically. "I'll stay in your chalet at night. I will, Mike. Half the students are doing much the same, anyway."

"What good will that do? Perhaps that's what she wants."

57

"I've brought this on you, haven't I? Why should she haunt you and not me?"

She was so pathetically distressed that it would have melted the heart of a nail, but I remained irritable.

"How the hell should I know?"

"Oh, please . . . You know there's nothing I wouldn't do . . ." She stared at the writing, looking so like a horrified cat that if she had had pointed ears she would have laid them back. " 'Draw me'," she whispered. "She means, draw Isabel."

"She can't make me," I said.

I spoke defiantly, but inside was dreadful weakness and the wish to give in. Isabel's shapely body, perched on the edge of the Common Room armchair, aroused me not physically, as it should have done, but with the craving to draw it. What I dreaded most, I longed to do. Addiction to a drug must be like this.

"We need help," I said.

"Who could help us?"

Suddenly, inspiration came to me out of the gloom. "Your Dr Diener might."

"He wouldn't look at me again. Anyway, got a fortune?"

"He might help us for nothing." And I told her what I'd read in the paper. "See? Supernatural experiences connected with art. If this isn't one, what is?"

"He's sweet, Dr Diener," said Isabel thoughtfully. "He's very understanding. I certainly would like his opinion."

"I'll find that paper and write to him."

"I've got his phone number, as it happens."

A female voice of extreme precision answered the phone. To speak to Dr Diener? it said, in a slight accent. No, that would not be possible. This was his secretary. She would take the message.

"Tell him I've seen a spirit-image, a double," I said.

"Three times. And twice it's made me paint a picture I had no intention of painting. And it's just left me a message in spirit-writing. Do you think he'll be interested?"

"One moment," said the voice, still precise, but with the professional calm of a beekeeper who has just knocked over a hive of bees. "You have seen, you say, a double? A *doppelgänger*?"

"Yes."

"Of yourself?"

"No, someone else's."

"Then it cannot be a true *doppelgänger*."

"Oh, sorry," I said, "perhaps it's gate-crashed. All I know is—"

"One moment. Is this a joke?"

"It certainly is not."

"Of that, how can I be certain?"

"Isabel Carrick," I said. "She was Dr Diener's patient about two years ago. This is her double. It's transferred itself to me."

"*Ach so*," said the voice, with a kindling of interest. "Isabel Carrick. Yes, the name is on our files. One moment, please."

She was gone so long that I had to put another coin in the box. "Isabel Carrick," she said, with a strain of disapproval. "Her parents discontinued the course."

"Unfortunately," I said, "her *doppelgänger* did not."

"One moment please."

She returned as I was inserting a third coin. "Yes, good," she said. "The Herr Doctor is interested. When can you call on him?"

"I can't call on him. I'm on an art course in Somerset. He'll have to call on me."

"That is impossible."

"Then he'll miss the scoop of a lifetime. There's something in the atmosphere of this *place*—"

"One moment. Isabel Carrick, is she with you on this course?"

"Yes, she is."

"One moment, please."

She returned after another protracted moment to take my name and the address of the college. "And look," I said, "this is urgent. We have only two weeks left of the course."

"*Jawohl*. Already I am booking local accommodation."

They came down to Newfield that very evening, to The Three Feathers, a three-star hotel at the other end of the village from the Abbey, and we met them in Dr Diener's room. They recognized Isabel, and the secretary, Miss Dummer, gave a little nod to confirm that this had clicked into place. She was not the ice-maiden I had expected, though, but a big, bunchy girl with a beefy face, and fussy, and full of concern.

As Isabel had described him as "sweet", I had expected Dr Diener to be round-faced and rubicund, with a halo of white hair and a charming, apologetic accent; but he was lean and lined, with tired grey eyes, and his English was immaculate, although too perfect to pass for an Englishman's. He spoke rapidly and precisely, ending each sentence like the closing of a door.

"There are tales of apparitions of living persons," he remarked, when he had heard our stories. "In wartime, women have seen images of their sons in uniform, when the young men were in the agony of battle. These cases have always occurred in moments of emotional stress."

This reminded us of Jenny O'Brien's grandmother, and the apparition of the little girl. "Jenny's very sceptical about it, though."

"Ah. She is too educated. Education develops the brain at the expense of the instincts. The most psychic people are often the most ignorant. Thus, in accounts of the supernatural, scientific truth is often confused with superstitious nonsense."

"You think that there is scientific truth, though?" said Isabel.

"I allow for its possibility. Now, you say that there is something special about the atmosphere of your college, Newfield Abbey?"

"I feel sure there is."

"Your Principal has kindly granted me permission to look round it. I shall like to meet this young tutor, Miss O'Brien, also. The story of her grandmother is very interesting."

"I saw *myself*," said Isabel.

"Yes. A *doppelgänger*."

"I've heard you use that word before, but you've never told me what they are."

"There are many theories. Remember, these are not my beliefs; I merely repeat what is told. They are sometimes said to be earth-bound spirits who have lost their way and want to rejoin the human world. They prey on human beings like parasites. They take the form of anyone they can fasten on to. Mirrors, photographs, portraits, are sometimes aids to them. I discuss this in my book."

"But what do they want?"

"To possess that person. To take him over, body and soul. To *become* that person. They are spirits looking for a body to lodge in."

Isabel shuddered. "That's it," she whispered. "You've told me what I know." But he leaned forward and looked into her eyes very earnestly.

"Remember this is only hypothesis. I repeat it. I do not say I subscribe to it."

"But you must think there's some truth in it, sir," I said, "or why are you writing your book?"

"I enquire," he said. "I enquire. Not enough is known. In this case, it is too early to make pronouncements."

"Too early?" I said. "We've got to go through a lot more of it?"

"Purely from the point of view of investigation, that would help."

"Great," I said glumly.

He turned his overworked eyes on me and smiled a thin, difficult smile.

"Let us suppose," he said, "for the sake of argument only, that this *doppelgänger* is not imaginary, that she does exist. You have great fear of her. Yet, the evidence suggests, she is not all-powerful. She is fallible."

"What do you mean?"

"Suppose you wished to burgle somebody's house. Would you knock on his door, wearing a mask? Would you not creep in unobserved? Your *doppelgänger*," he said to Isabel, "wishes to burgle *you*, as it were. Why then should she advertise the fact by appearing in a mirror using a comb when you were using brushes? To frighten you? Why should she wish to do that? Would that serve her purpose? On the contrary, it warned you against her. The fact is, she made a slip, somehow. She didn't get your image quite right. You see? She makes mistakes."

"And could be defeated," I said.

"And could be defeated, as, we are told, all evil spirits can be."

"Isabel baffled her for a while with her drawings," I said.

"That, to me, is the most fascinating part of your tale, but I cannot understand it, as yet."

"Anyway, she's transferred herself to me."

"No. She cannot do that, any more than one human being can transfer to another. She has taken Isabel's form. Isabel is her goal. She is using you, she intends to work through you, but she is not your *doppelgänger*."

"How?" I demanded. "How will she use me?"

The secretary, Miss Dummer, looked up briefly, and for a fraction I thought she seemed uneasy. Dr Diener was silent for a long time, his face dark and working. "I cannot say," he said. "It would be speculating about a speculation. I cannot say."

I suspected that, as a matter of fact, he could. An obscene and nameless fear crept into my mind.

Isabel did not, as it happened, stay in my chalet at nights. This move looks easy on television, but is often difficult to arrange in real life. She was not brazen enough to invade the wholly male province of the chalets at bed-time, when the other boys were about (and neither were any of the other girls, whatever they got up to elsewhere) nor brave enough to steal through the dark and silent woods at a later time. I was relieved. I was human, and could feel excited at the thought of spending a night with her, but not with the risks involved. Dr Diener had said, "Isabel is the *doppelgänger*'s goal." It might be like bringing a lamb to the sacrifice, and I was not forgetting that I might get butchered as well.

Isabel was very scared on my account, and so was I. Apart from anything else, my imagination was playing me tricks. When I lay in bed, and closed my eyes, I saw faces on my eyelids. Sometimes they were the faces Isabel had drawn, but they always twisted out of shape, as if they were melting; they became Isabel, and then her double, with her black glasses; and then the glasses would be lifted off, but I never actually saw her eyes. I would snap my eyes open and sit up with a gasp; and then that deep and heavy sleep would overtake me and I would lapse into it, as if I were drugged.

9 Isabel was not so fortunate; she slept badly. People who noticed the anxious consultations that took place between us every morning may well have jumped to the wrong conclusions.

"What will become of us, Mike? We've got less than a fortnight here. What will happen then?"

"We'll write and ring each other up and meet as often as possible. We'll go on doing that for years until we get married. Then we'll stay married, because if ever two people were meant for each other, we are."

"I wish I had your confidence," said Isabel wryly. "What about *her*?"

"We'll get rid of her."

"How? You think, love will find a way, sort of thing?"

"Yes, I do."

"Well, I think," said Isabel, "that we may be poison to each other. I think we may be playing into her hands. I think she can destroy us both."

There was a sort of authority of despair in her tone, and it chilled me. But I rallied.

"Even if I wanted to pack it in, I couldn't. You know that's true."

"Yes." She was slightly consoled. "You keep those drawings of mine about you, don't you?"

But even this mystic precaution was soon to be discredited. Dr Diener turned up that morning, accompanied by

64

the faithful Miss Dummer, and as soon as I could get a word with him I asked him whether the drawings could have any effect.

"None whatever."

"They work for Isabel."

"I have thought about that. This is different. I shall explain.—You realize, of course, that all this is mere fanciful conjecture, and that I do not necessarily—"

"Yes, yes."

"Yes. Those drawings are creations of Isabel's. She projected herself into them. They are something other than herself. The *doppelgänger* cannot identify with them. They bar her way. But only to Isabel herself. Not to you."

"Not to me."

"You might as well lock someone else's door to stop entry to your own house."

"So," I said, trying to grasp this, "I would have to make my own drawings?"

"Yes."

"A drawing of Isabel herself would help the double?"

"It would be to its maximum advantage. Or so," said Dr Diener, with his unvaried caution, "so those who accept the existence of *doppelgängers* would have us believe."

"But how, sir? Would she step through the picture or something? She has already materialized to me, she's quite solid. How could she materialize any more?"

"No, she would not step through the picture to you. Her motive would be to make you step through the picture to her."

And once more, Dr Diener required me to remember that this was not proven science, it belonged in the realm of witchcraft, there might be no truth in it. I was not reassured.

I had wondered, incidentally, what excuse he had given the Principal for visiting the college, roaming through its grounds, and browsing through its archives. Miss Dummer gravely explained this to me. He had told the Principal that the

65

Abbey, being very old, was a storehouse of legends he would like to investigate, and the Principal, being primarily a businessman, like most principals, had welcomed this eminent and painstaking German because he foresaw some free publicity. He did not know that the legend that interested Dr Diener was, as far as the college was concerned, only two weeks old.

The next day Dr Diener, having completed his enquiries, went back to his busy life in London. "If there are any further developments, ring me," he said. "I wish to keep in touch with your case. You understand, of course, it would not be like calling an ambulance. I cannot guarantee a cure."

"Usually," Miss Dummer assured me, "the Herr Doctor charges high fees for such services."

"I'm honoured," I said. It seemed to me that I was first-rate copy for his book. But Miss Dummer did not perceive my sarcasm. She nodded with satisfaction. Honoured. *Ja*.

Jenny liked him. I think he must have adjusted to everyone he spoke to, because she supposed him to be as sceptical as herself. He spoke to her of auto-suggestion and the powers of the mind. He knew a great deal about art, and they discussed surrealism and other far-out movements. "A most interesting man," she said. "What a pity he has to spend his time on neurotics."

She was rather hard, Jenny. She had almost as little time for nerves as she had for the supernatural. Yet lately, she herself had been pale and rather moody. She admitted that she did not feel well. "I'm sickening for something, I expect," she said. "No, I don't need any time off. I'll be all right."

When the Doctor had gone, Isabel said to me, "Well, are you any the wiser?"

"I've learned a bit about *doppelgängers*. Assuming that they exist, of course, and that your double isn't just someone dressed up in a sheet. There's so much that I don't
66

understand, though. Why should Elizabeth have to use another person to get at you?"

"I think, because I can resist her. I think she can't persuade me against my will. It's supposed to be the same with hypnotism. They say people won't do what hypnotists tell them to, unless they want to, basically."

"How am I going to help her?"

"I've no idea. But I thought Dr Diener *might* have one."

"Yes, me too." I brooded for a while. "Maybe you're right. Maybe we are bad for each other. Maybe we should break up."

I wanted her to make a noble speech about loving each other for ever, such as I'd made to her, but she didn't respond.

"She wouldn't let us," she said flatly.

"There's another thing I don't understand," I said. "*The* thing. However did she take your appearance in the first place? How did she materialize as Libby?"

"I've often, often wondered that. She was around for a long time before I actually saw her."

"That still doesn't—"

"No, Mike," said Isabel, with mild impatience. "The thing about mysteries is that they mystify you. All we can do is play this by ear. But one thing we can and will do—we'll take all your drawing things out of your chalet: everything, Mike, pens and pencils and every scrap of paper, and move them into the cupboard in the hall. You say you have this weird urge to draw me, and I can just see her making you do so some night. O.K.?"

"Like taking a smoker's cigarettes away from him?"

"Yes, right."

"Whatever would Jenny say?"

"Jenny doesn't know the half of it. She's not been looking too good lately, have you noticed?"

"She says she sickening for something."

"Love, perhaps," said Isabel, quite maliciously.

The students were allotted some cupboard room at the back of the hall, where we kept all our larger material, and I now collected everything from my chalet that could make or receive a mark, including even a packet of cartridges for my pen, and moved it into this space. My drawing-board was in there, with four or five drawings pinned to it, all false starts, because my work was going through a bad patch. It fretted me, because there was to be a final exhibition at the end of the course, and I had nothing prepared. I was distracted. I won't say that everything I drew tried to turn into Isabel, but whenever I set to work the compulsion to draw her was so strong that it paralysed the attempt to draw anything else.

Everyone thought, I expect, that my much-praised still life had been a flash in the pan. Jenny reassured me: "Don't worry. Not all the drawings can be good ones." I knew that there was one, which would be very good, that I mustn't draw. But time goes on however you feel, and I got through the day somehow, and had to face the night again.

Isabel clung and clung to me before letting me go, but we parted quite early, and I went to bed amid the comforting noise of other students turning in. Oh, how I envied them! They might think they had troubles, but they had nothing like mine.

Once more I fell heavily asleep, but this night I dreamed of the child again. There was the great, dark, bleak room, with the two people dead in the corner, and the child in panic; once again their identity kept changing; once again there was the terror of being abandoned and lost. Once again the din raged outside. But this time, through the foul chaos of sound, a single word began to make itself clear. It was my name: Michael, Michael, Michael . . .

I woke up, and sat up, panting, relieved to be awake, and trying to clear my head of the memory of the nightmare. There was a hush, as if its racket had been switched off. And then I realized that something had stayed on from the dream. It was the sound of my name: Michael, Michael . . .

It came from just outside my chalet door, and the voice was Isabel's. At first I thought that she had kept her word at last and turned up to spend the night with me. But no, it was not her voice. It was an impersonation: it was too sibilant, it had a false sweetness, a faked innocence. It was like the voice of a doll. It was sickening. It drew me like a quicksand.

I switched on the light, dragged some clothes on, unbolted my door and threw it wide. The light from my chalet struck bushes and trees. A small rain was falling, and I saw its fine needles slanting in the light. But that was all. I waited for the figure of Elizabeth to slide from the trees into my view. Nothing came.

I was sure she was there. I could feel she was there. Once before, on this path, I had had the feeling of being accompanied, but this was twice as strong. This was so strong that it drew me from my chalet as though I were manacled to an invisible gaoler, and guided me along the path in the darkness towards the main drive.

There was only one thing worse than seeing Isabel's double, and that was not seeing her. To see her gave you something to focus on. This blind obedience was dreadful. I cursed into the darkness and snarled at her: "Show yourself." I felt her defiance. It was as if she had pursed her lips and folded her arms against me. I felt her revelling in it.

I no longer heard her voice, although it echoed inside my head: Michael, Michael. I reached the main drive, and the point where it curved past the girls' rooms on the ground floor. I passed Isabel's curtained window. I wanted to knock on it, to shout something to her, a warning or a cry for help, but I could not, and I went on. Suddenly, a poison of hatred filled me. Isabel, of all people, was spared this ordeal. Ever since we had been down here, I had been the haunted one; I was her scapegoat, her witch doctor. My whole being raged against her. I hated her.

I reached the Abbey porch, where a light was kept on all night, and opened the huge oak door. It creaked, as doors do in horror films. I went into the great hall, and down the corridor, and into the room where the exhibition had been held. In pitch darkness, but without trouble, I opened the cupboard at the back, and took out my drawing-board and a case of pencils. I went to the small classroom where I had drawn Jenny, switched on the light, laid my drawing-board on a table, turned over a few sheets of paper, and took up a pencil.

I began drawing with an ease I had never known in my life before. As I drew, it was as if my spirit left my body, and stood back watching my hand at work. I needed no model. In a cool intensity of concentration I worked on the hair, and the lines of the throat, and the cheeks, and the mouth.

And then, with a strange swooping feeling and a punch of the heart, I was one with my body again; and, on an impulse I cannot explain, I abandoned the face and began filling in the background. And as I shaded it in, I thought of that cavernous room in my dream, and of the pitiful little child, and my hatred for Isabel was overtaken by a flood of compassion and remorse. I knew that I was doing a terrible thing. I was betraying her. This outline of a drawing was like her body on a sacrificial stone. For the first time, I felt Elizabeth's command of me waver.

Her voice sounded in my ear, poisonously sweet in persuasion:

"Michael: *put in the eyes*."

Instead I flung my pencil across the room, ripped the paper from the board, and tore it across and across again and again. Each time I tore it I was slashed with pain as if with blows from a stockwhip. I crammed the wad of torn fragments into my pocket and stood shuddering and on the point of vomiting.

The air about me was filled with an overpowering reek of

fury and hatred, the distillation of the poison that had filled myself, but ten times as strong. Yet I felt no fear, because I sensed that the thing present was as powerless to hurt me as a dog chained to a wall. Something, some force of which I had no conception, had intervened when I had been on the brink of destruction, and Elizabeth, this time at least, had failed.

I stood for a while in a collapse of relief as the foul odour of evil faded. The room was normal. I collected my things together, switched off the light, went into the exhibition room and restored them to the cupboard. I was free. My tormentor had gone.

I heard footsteps in the corridor outside, very slow and uncertain. I shrank back into the corner of the room and waited for them to pass. To be found here at this hour of the night would be awkward, and I had no explanation that anyone would believe. I had not thought that the light in the classroom might be spotted.

Yet it was odd that whoever had come to investigate should be groping his way in the dark. There was no light under the door. The footsteps continued unsteady. They passed the door, and went on to the classroom I had just left.

I crept out into the corridor, almost to collide with the maker of the footsteps. It was Jenny.

Her eyes were wide open, but she did not see me. There is something frightening about a sleepwalker. I had heard it said that it is dangerous to wake them. I did not mean to try. She wavered for a moment, standing there in her dressing gown within inches of me; then she went back down the corridor and up the stairs to the tutors' rooms.

10 Jenny, we were told the next morning, was in the sick-bay, having at last yielded to whatever she was sickening for and given herself up to the nursing sister. "She's working for a second degree in her spare time," said the tutor who stood in for her, "and she's let herself get run down."

"She looks as strong as a horse," said Isabel.

"Ah, but she's been overdoing it. She's been keeping very late nights."

"Yes," I said, automatically, but carelessly, for Isabel pounced on it as soon as we were alone.

"What did you mean, *yes*? How do you know what hours she keeps?"

"She—er—told me she stayed up late."

"Oh. She confides in you, does she?"

I hadn't yet found the courage to tell her about the events of the night, and she, although her usual anxious self, clearly had no inkling of them. Although I felt guilty, I myself was exceptionally relaxed. I felt as though I were temporarily off duty, like a soldier on leave from war. In the lunch-hour, seizing a moment when Isabel was called to the phone, I paid Jenny a visit. I wondered how I should look *her* in the eye, too, but she showed no recollection of what she had done. She was cheerful, as people often are when they give in to illness and rest. She sat up in bed, eating grapes and grinning at me. She was such a practical, *daylight* person, Jenny, that I almost wondered whether *I* had been the sleepwalker and imagined it.

"This is very sweet of you, Michael. It's my own silly fault, so it is." (This was a bit of stage Irish for fun. Jenny retained traces of her accent, however, in a voice that made me feel that my own was filleted of all music.) "And how's yourself? You're looking better than you did a day or two ago."

"I'm all right."

"And how's Deirdre of the Sorrows today?" She burst out laughing at my sullen response. "Oh, I shouldn't tease you. I know you're head over heels about her."

"Jenny," I said, "he jests at scars who never felt a wound. To coin a phrase."

"Yes," she said, sobering. "It's just that when I think of what's happening in the world—in my own poor country, for instance—I find it hard to take her kind of wounds seriously."

"All the same," I said, "I'm afraid that most people cry more tears over their own affairs than over other people's massacres. Like, over broken love affairs. Or even toothache."

"O wise young judge!" said Jenny. "She's lucky to have you. I hope you'll always think yourself lucky to have her. No, no, I do *not* dislike her; she's gifted, and of course, I realize she's the dishiest thing . . . It's just that—well, she's a poor little rich girl, Michael, with nothing to think about but herself. Everything's always been done for her, and you may find that you'll have to carry her as well as yourself. There, now. I think I can get away with murder if I take to my bed and put on an Irish accent, don't I?"

"I know what you mean," I said. Yes, did I not! She was nearer to the truth than she could have known.

"So, forgive me for being rude?"

"Seeing you're an invalid."

"Come here, then."

I went up to her and she gave me a kiss like the bursting of a sky-rocket. "Take care now," she said.

I was not so relaxed that I forgot what Dr Diener had said, and several times during the day I tried to phone him to tell him of the latest development. It was not easy to get to the phone, because Isabel seemed more strung-up than ever and was suspicious of my every move; and when I did get to it he was absent every time. People on the stage come in on their cues. Real life is more ragged.

I think I must have been what Americans call "in shock" that day, for I felt so little after-effect, when I should have felt, almost, as if I had returned from the grave. We say such things as "I lost my wits"; "my heart was in my mouth"; well, I had felt like that in real earnest. I had been divided into two selves, one watching the other, and I honestly believe that for a few moments I had been on the brink of hell. But today I simply couldn't feel it; I was half-prepared to believe it had been a dream. Jenny's cheerful mockery seemed to express the real world. The obsession to draw Isabel was lifted. My work returned to normal, and I managed "nude, reclining" quite satisfactorily for the exhibition.

When the afternoon session was over, Isabel insisted on going for a walk.

"Where are we going?"

"Anywhere."

She was not in a good mood, and we walked to the top of the drive in a constrained silence. As we went out into the road she said, "You're invited home for the week-end. Can you endure it?"

"That's very kind of—"

"Oh, don't be polite. She only wants you for further inspection. To see how we react to each other. Like a zoo-keeper hoping the pandas will mate."

"You're hard on your mother."

74

"Yes, I blame her for everything."

"Is that fair?"

"Who wants to be fair?"

"I don't think you should blame your parents for everything. What about if they blame their parents?"

"Oh, she does. Her mother went mad when she got divorced."

"She's been under a lot of strain in her time—"

"Are you training to be a social worker? Whose side are you on?"

"I do know that you have a tremendous emotional stranglehold on your mother—"

"Oh, don't *nag*! Do you realize what a prig you sound?"

So ended my feeble attempt at arbitration. We walked further in silence, till Isabel, regretting her outburst of temper, began taking sidelong glances at me, while I stared straight ahead, hoping she would make an overture, so that I could repulse it. We reached the church, and went, of all places, into the cemetery, and sat down on a bench alone among the graves.

"How was Jenny?" asked Isabel tentatively.

"Getting better," I said, and added, meanly, "She kissed me."

"Very nice," said Isabel wanly. "I said there was an affinity between you."

I was sick of this, and suddenly felt tender for her. "Sod affinity," I said. "I love you."

This she must have assumed for some time, but it was the first time I had said the words. The effect was startling; she turned away and covered her face, and sobbed as if her heart would break. I put my arm round her, but she pushed it away and went on shaking with sobs until they turned into splashes and sniffs which she mopped up with a tissue. She said, between subsiding sniffs:

"Well, you mustn't. You mustn't. You mustn't."

Then she became quite calm. "Mike," she said, "do you know how Elizabeth is going to use you? I've thought and thought about it and now I know. Dr Diener knows, and that German girl, that Miss Dummer, she knows too. And now I wonder how I could have been so dense."

"I'm still dense, I'm afraid—"

"I see I've got to tell you about the birds and bees." She sounded almost flippant, but her air of drooping wretchedness belied it. "First, she means to take your spirit, possess you . . ."

I thought of that awful separation of myself from myself, and I froze. "And what then?"

"Mike, *you* want to possess *me*, don't you? Some time?"

"Yes, of course, of course I do. What do you think it's all about? But—"

"But what? But you're willing to wait, like a gentleman? For years? Till we get married, even? Mike, she can wait, too. She left me alone for nine years once. Don't you see what I'm getting at?" She stared into my face, and said with complete composure, "I'm afraid you're my worst enemy, my love."

"God," I said. I understood.

I still hadn't told her of the previous night, and now I couldn't find the heart to do so. I sat feeling as though the universe had collapsed around me.

And then I remembered the mysterious force that had come to my aid last night at the very last moment when I had been on the verge of completing the drawing. I couldn't tell her of this without telling her everything, But I did pull myself together sufficiently to say:

"Dr Diener says that evil spirits can always be defeated."

"It seems to me this one's winning."

"She's not going to win. We'll find a way of beating her."

"Oh, Mike, how will you know, when you think you're doing the right thing, that you're not just playing into her hands? Why did you fall in love with me in the first place? Mike, she got there first! She *chose* you, Mike . . ."

11 It is disturbing to suspect that you have fallen in love with a *doppelgänger* when you have supposed yourself to be in love with a girl. This was not something my parents had reckoned with when they had paid the fees for the course.

However, Isabel's double was passive for a while, and I began to recover my nerve. It was a silence full of mischief, no doubt, but I was grateful for any relief. All that troubled me, the next night, and the night after, and the night after that, was the dream, that same dream of the great dark room and the terrified child. With that strange knowledge peculiar to dreams, I seemed to have known this child all my life. It was the same child that looked through the railings in the drawing of Isabel's garden. It was also myself, Isabel, and every frightened child everywhere. It was getting more and more distressed. The background—the bodies in the corner and all the features of the room—was receding now, and the child itself was coming into focus, and I was waiting for its sobbing and whimpering to turn into words. The dream moved me more and more. I would even wake up to find myself in tears. But it was an immense relief to be awake.

My relationship with Isabel was changed. Now and then she would clutch me tragically and hold me for a few moments in a frantic hug, but most of the time she fended me off, acting cheerful and comradely, so that our situation was like that desperately unsatisfactory one when a girl tells you that she cannot love you any more but wants to go on being friends. But it made talking easier, in some ways, and after a couple of days I managed to tell her of how I had almost drawn her picture, and all the details of that night.

She was less shocked, or more understanding, than I had expected. "Hated me, did you?" she said. "Shows you have some feeling for me, anyway. So what was this mysterious thing that changed your mind for you? Love Conquering All?" She tried to sound cynical, but she was hoping I would say yes, I think. I could not oblige.

"No, not that at all. Something quite outside myself. Something else."

"You were wearing your anorak. My drawing?"

"No, Dr Diener says that's rubbish."

"What then? An angel? God?"

"I tell you, I don't know."

"Nice to know something's on our side, anyway."

"I must say you've taken this very well. I expected an attack on Jenny."

"Ah, but I didn't, did I?" Isabel cogitated for a few moments. "No, no, you couldn't possibly connect . . . It's very strange, though, that she should be sleepwalking at the same time that—"

"Oh, it's the other way round: I was doing my thing at the same time that she was sleepwalking. There's nothing unusual in sleepwalking. It's no odder than that she should have migraines."

"No . . . Goodness, that strapping wench is more of a wreck than she looks, isn't she?"

"Aren't we all?" I said, with feeling. "I'm going to ring Dr Diener again. This ought to go into his casebook."

I feared that Dr Diener might have had all he needed from us—our case would probably fill only about half a page in his enormous tome—but I misjudged him. He was like those archaeologists who will shift tons of rubble in the hope of finding one small fragment of pottery. He left no stone unturned. Not only did he agree to come down, but he actually booked rooms at The Three Feathers for the duration of the course.

"The Herr Doctor," Miss Dummer told me, "is exceedingly thorough in his researches."

"I'll say," I said. "How does his wife take his going off like this?"

"He has no wife."

"Oh, a bachelor."

"Precisely, not. He has been married three times, already. Unfortunately, all his marriages broke down because he was always so busy counselling people."

Surely Miss Dummer was not being ironical? She was much too pink and earnest.

This little chat took place in the college, because Dr Diener's first call, surprisingly, was on Jenny O'Brien, who was confined to the sick-bay for the rest of the week, although outwardly glowing with health.

"Did you tell him about her sleepwalking?" asked Isabel.

"Well, I told Miss Dummer, on the phone. I think it's carrying thoroughness a bit far."

"Perhaps he's looking for a fourth wife."

Our meeting with the doctor, however, again took place in his room in the hotel, with extra chairs brought in from Miss Dummer's room and arranged between the television set and the dressing-table. Dr Diener had the same air of scholarly weariness, but he was less inclined this time to hedge himself round with cautious warnings about fantasy and conjecture. He went straight to the point.

He asked Isabel: "Did you ever visit the Abbey before you came on this course?"

"Yes, we came down a week before, to enrol. My mother wanted to see what the place was like. Why?"

"It might explain why, on the day the course began, your *doppelgänger* arrived three hours before you did, and appeared to this young man. No? She found, perhaps, that the Abbey suited her? Now, why should she find that it suited her? Was it the atmosphere? The place is very old. But if it was the atmosphere, why has no one else noticed it? Your fellow students live very close to you, yet they have not the faintest idea of what is happening to you. Your story would astonish them." He turned to me. "Tell me again of what happened the other night."

I told him, and he made me repeat it yet again, in careful detail.

"You went to this classroom, you made a drawing, you tore it up. You saw nothing; you think you heard something; you sensed some power that came to your aid. You returned to your chalet. You could have been moved solely by your imagination, no? It could have been 'all in the mind', could it not?"

"That's what anyone would tell me, yes."

"Please—forgive me—I wish to hear once again of how you felt that your spirit left your body."

I wondered whether he was trying to catch me out. I went over it yet again, hoping that I was not contradicting myself.

"The belief that the spirit can leave the body," said Dr Diener, "is held by many races. Miss Dummer has listed some of them for me."

Miss Dummer, who had been writing notes in shorthand with ease and speed, put down her pencil and began a prompt recital, sounding like a recorded telephone message.

"The Itonamas of South America," she announced, "used to seal up the eyes, nose and mouth of a dying person, in case the soul should escape and carry off others. In Transylvania a person must not sleep with his mouth open, or his soul may slip out in the form of a bird or mouse. The Minangkabauers believe that the soul always leaves the body in sleep. The

80

Bataks of Sumatra believe that the soul can leave the body in sickness, great fright, or distress. The Karens believe that the soul can be abducted by demons, ghosts, or sorcerers. The Kawiri tribe of Southern Borneo believe—"

"Thank you, Miss Dummer," said Dr Diener.

"These beliefs are not common in Redhill," I remarked. "They believe in life insurance."

Miss Dummer looked up. "Please?"

"The young man means that the people in his community have a materialistic outlook," explained Dr Diener. "They place their trust in financial security."

"*Ach so*," said Miss Dummer, with satisfaction, and made a note. "An idiom. To believe in life insurances."

"You will say, these are the superstitions of primitive peoples," said Dr Diener. "They seem to us very absurd. Are they in fact so absurd? Is it possible that these people, in their ignorance, are giving childlike explanations to things that really exist?—as they do to the sun, the moon and the stars? Might not our own way of life have blinded us to these things?"

"How does all this apply to me?" asked Isabel.

"Listen very carefully.

"As a very young child, you overheard bitter quarrels between your parents. You were too young to understand them, but you were all the more terrified. You wanted your mother. Your spirit sought your mother for comfort—"

"Like Jenny O'Brien's mother when the school caught fire," said Isabel.

"Yes. But your mother, unlike the mother of Miss O'Brien, was not psychic, and did not see you. You ran for help, and you received no reply.

"There was fear and hatred in your house. Where there is fear and hatred, evil spirits are always present. One such spirit caught this part of you which could not reach your mother, and would not let it return to you."

"And became Libby," said Isabel.

"And became Libby. Now it has contact with you. Now it can appear as your body. It has become a *doppelgänger*. But its desire is *to become you*. It must find a way to take your whole person over. For years, it waits for its opportunity.

"A young man arrives at the Abbey on whom the *doppelgänger* decides to fix. This young man now has a role to play. He has become a go-between. Do you understand the significance of this?"

Miss Dummer looked up. "Eventually, excuse me," she said to me, "you will wish to give Isabel a baby, or at least—"

"Yes, I've got the point," I said.

"It is all very inexact, all fantasy, perhaps," said Dr Diener, in his tired, unemphatic voice. "We are doing no better than the Karens or the Bataks of Sumatra. If we are right, one thing is certain. Your *doppelgänger* will never give up of its own accord. You must quell it. You must defeat it."

"And how do we go about that, sir?" I asked.

"We have not yet arrived at the answer."

Did he care about us as human beings? Or were we just interesting data? He must have guessed my thoughts, for he gave me his tight smile.

"Perhaps we shall not arrive at it," he said. "Remember what I said about being too educated. Perhaps reason will not help. You spoke of some force that intervened when you were doing the drawing. Eventually perhaps it will make itself better known."

12 Isabel and I walked slowly up the college drive.

"I wonder if I'd have done better," she said, "to have been brought up in a hovel with a pig running in and out, like Jenny?"

"If Jenny heard that, she'd slosh you."

"She can't have it both ways. She thinks I've been brought up in a cocoon. What should I do about it? Drop out? All drop-outs really do is find some other set of mugs to lean on."

"Well, never mind."

"My being haunted by Elizabeth," said Isabel, "is a judgement on my mother. She's the one who made the cocoon. But she couldn't protect me against Elizabeth. Elizabeth's not in her world. Literally."

"It's no good guessing what you might have been," I said. "It's what you are that you've got to deal with."

"Mike, you ought to compile calendars. You know, with a Great Thought for every day."

"If I did, it would be a pussy-cat one, with you hissing on the cover."

She was in a bitchy mood because we were going to her parents, but she never stayed bitchy for long. She quite liked being hit back at.

"You're always comparing me to a cat. I hope you like cats."

"I hope you," I said, "are not going to make snide remarks all weekend. It's too embarrassing."

83

The gleaming bulk of Malcolm's car rolled into view, silent except for the obsequious whisper of the dust under its wheels. He got out and opened the rear door for us.

"And how are you, young fellow?"

"The name's Michael," said Isabel.

Once again, I felt sorry for him. He had worked hard all his life and had nothing to show for it, except a lot of money. His wife had grown indifferent to him and Isabel was persistently rude, and he remained polite and cheerful through it all. I imagined him making allowances for their being female. I could hear him saying, tolerantly, "You know what women are." That might not be a masterpiece of insight, but I respected him for it, and so I leaned forward in the rear seat and made myself as pleasant as possible. Isabel watched me, smiling. It was funny, but she seemed pleased that I was being nice to Malcolm. It was as if she felt herself under some obligation to be rude to him, and was glad to be relieved of it.

I started off with the weather, and this got us on to the subject of gardening. I was handicapped, because I only knew three flowers, and two of them were roses, but I must have sounded enthusiastic, because he promised to show me over his garden when we arrived.

Which he did. The front part I knew already, of course, but the garden at the back of the house stretched as far as the eye could see, magnificent, the sort that television gardeners would give a programme to. It sloped up a hillside, but Malcolm had levelled it off in terraces, step after step, in green plateaux up to the height. This grassy expanse was flanked by flowerbeds with side-paths at intervals, and when we turned left into one of these we were faced by a rockery about as high as the Mappin Terraces, with a cascade of colour down it, starry bits of white and pink and blue, with a dominant motif of yellow.

"Alpine calceolarias," said Malcolm, stroking one of the yellow flowers as he might the cheek of a baby. "Easy to grow.

Hardy. Look behind you." I did, to see a bed just clear of the rockery, a mass of small pink flowers, broken up here and there with other things with long narrow green blades. "Know what they are? Busy Lizzie! Grown from seed. Spider plants among them."

I felt bound to say something. "I love the way you've hung those roses on ropes in the front."

"Ah! I pinched that idea from the Horticultural Gardens. Do you like these?" These were daisy-like flowers with orange petals and dark-brown centres. "Gazania. One of my favourites. Annuals, of course."

Through these bits of rather grunting speech I could sense his passion for his garden. His heart was here; it was his refuge from the phoney world of human affection. It renewed itself for him with every season, fresh and lovely. He paid people to do the hard work, of course, but he was its creator, and what a success he had made of it! And, I thought, he'd made a success of everything else, too: his business, even his marriage. He had kept his part of the bargain. It was the others who had not lived up to it. All very well for Isabel to sneer at his "paying his way". Why shouldn't he give a donation to the college? Could she think of anything they'd like more? I could understand his winning her mother away from her first husband—again, by donations, I didn't doubt. He might not be Isabel's taste in men but he was fair by his own standards. He paid his way.

"We'll go in now, shall we?" he said. "Don't want to bore you."

"No, I think it's terrific."

"Just hard work, really, and keep at it."

When we went in I said, unnecessarily, "I've been seeing your garden."

"Yes," said Isabel brightly. "Isn't it a lovesome thing, God wot?"

She was quoting from some poem, I think, a pretty awful one, if that were a typical line. Her parents laughed and treated it as a joke, but as soon as we were alone I challenged her.

"For my sake, lay off, will you?"

"All right," she said meekly. "I'm sorry, Mike—that garden may be a paradise for Malcolm, but for me it's an extension of prison. So far from the road, see?"

"All the same—"

"All right, I'll be good."

And she was. We talked art with the Harpers, mainly. Mrs Harper knew quite a lot about it. We had dinner. We watched a bit of TV. The evening went by quite peaceably.

I looked down from my bedroom window into the garden. Rain was falling under a watery sky, with the moon discolouring the clouds like a petrol stain. It was a spectral, misty scene, and I could imagine Elizabeth coming slowly towards me down those grassy levels, shrouded like a vampire, and raising that white face to stare at me.

However, I got into bed, and was soon asleep, and this time I did not dream. But I woke again quite soon, and now I entered into that peculiar state where you allow a dream to run, even though you know you are awake. I let myself believe that I was in the enormous room of my dream, high and echoing and full of shadows, and I was sure that in one of the corners lay the corpses. My mind could not pick out any details in this room, but it knew instinctively the height and depth and atmosphere of it. All that was missing was the noise.

And then indeed I did hear a noise. It came in little scurries of sound which stopped and began again, drew near, retreated; and accompanying it I could now hear the panting and whimpering of the child. For several minutes it kept up these sudden, panicky little dashes, sounding all the while more and more frightened, till its whimpering became frantic sobs. I was terrified that It would collide with my bed

86

and perhaps climb on to it. Afraid of a small child crying to be comforted? The child was not of this earth and yes, I was afraid. If it should chance to touch me I thought I should die. And all this, mind you, while I knew quite well that I was in an ordinary, comfortable bedroom, and could destroy the whole illusion by pulling the light switch.

At last I did so. The bedroom sprang into the clarity of electric light, and there was no child, nor corpses, nor cavernous recesses. I tried not very successfully to be angry with myself.

I switched the light off, and, as if synchronized, the crying of the child began again, not in the room this time, but down below, in the garden. I had not imagined it. A trick of sound had transferred it to the wrong place, that was all. I went over and opened the window wide, and felt the crying draw me towards itself. It was irresistible. But this was not Elizabeth's evil attractive power. It was quite different; it appealed to my heart and called to the caring side of me. I had no choice but to go to it. I dressed quickly, and crept out to the landing.

Unsure of myself in this strange house, I groped my way to the head of the stairs and began to edge down them. When I was halfway down I made out someone moving in the hall.

"Isabel!"

I was so startled that my whisper almost broke into a cry. I gripped her and held her. "Can you hear it too?"

"It's so sad," she whispered back.

"It's a dream," I said distractedly. She seemed not to hear. She took my hand, led me into the kitchen, unlocked the outer door and opened it. Pitter-patter, pitter-patter, out there in the rain, we could hear the little feet, and the quick frightened breathing, and the high whine of whimpering.

She turned up the collar of her raincoat and stepped into the garden. Scared, helpless, at a loss, I followed her. It was all so strange, there was such a sense of enchantment, that I even wondered whether my spirit was wandering, and hers

87

too, so that our bodies still lay upstairs like the corpses in my dream; but I felt the rain in my hair and I knew I was there in physical fact. Hand in hand, we groped around the enormous garden. We brushed against dripping hedges and bushes; we climbed the soaking plateaux of grass. And always near, but never near enough, we heard the whimpering of the child: ahead of us, behind, to one side or the other.

Then, as though it were tired, or giving up defeated, the sound began to fade, until we were left standing in the rain unable to hear it at all. Isabel would not give up at once, but dragged me wretchedly from point to point until at last she realized the futility of it, and we stumbled back to the kitchen porch and clung to each other there, soaked and shaking.

"Mike! What was it? What *was* it?"

What indeed? All I knew was that the child who had appeared first in a dream had got more and more sharply into focus until it had stepped out of the dream and into the waking world.

I knew that it was linked like a Siamese twin to Elizabeth, Isabel's double.

I knew in fact that *there was not one spirit, there were two, and they were in conflict, like forces of good and evil.*

I knew that this child was the force that had prevented me from completing the drawing.

Strong, then. Yes, but not strong enough. Crying aloud for help.

All this I knew in my senses, but in the present situation I could not begin to put it into words. I held Isabel tight and said:

"Whatever it was it called to both of us. It's brought us together. It's good and it's on our side."

"It was so *sad*," she said, inconsolably.

13 I was awakened next morning by Malcolm, bringing
me a cup of tea.

"Sleeping the sleep of the just," he grunted affably.

"Good Heavens, is that the time?"

"Thought we'd let you sleep on. Isabel's only just woken
up, too. Overwork you on the course, do they?"

Isabel. I sat up and sipped my tea and doubted my sanity.
Or at least, I wasn't certain whether or not I had dreamt it all.
And then I spotted my anorak hanging over a chair. Large
black patches of wetness covered it, drying whitely round the
edges.

Isabel tiptoed in.

"Mike, it did happen, didn't it?"

"My soaking anorak says it did," I replied, pointing.

"Oh, what a relief! I was afraid I might have just walked in
my sleep, like Jenny . . . Mike, that was *not* Elizabeth leading
us around."

"No. The kid was calling to us *in spite of* Elizabeth."

In a lost and wondering voice Isabel said: "It was the little
girl who broke the teacup."

"It was the child in my dream," I said.

"It was the child we both put in our drawings of the
garden." Isabel held her head in her hands. "Oh, however
shall we sort it out? And whoever would believe us? I can
understand Jenny's attitude, I can really. But it's real all the
same, isn't it? And it gets worse."

I thought so too, but I tried to pretend otherwise. "No, it gets better. I tell you, that kid is on our side. And it's getting stronger, getting nearer to us."

"Mike," said Isabel, "you're a blessing. You're so optimistic. I love you."

At this moment, of all moments, her mother's voice called querulously from below: "Isabel! Breakfast!"

With a grimace at me, Isabel went downstairs. I followed her shortly afterwards to run into a minor tiff between Malcolm and Mrs Harper. Their hall was carpeted wall to wall in silver grey, and Mrs Harper had just found some muddy footprints on it. Fortunately, the indefatigable Malcolm had been doing some chore outdoors earlier this morning, and he was being blamed for them.

"You might have taken your shoes off when you came in!"

"Thought I did."

"It doesn't look like it, does it?"

"All right, I'll Hoover it."

"No, leave it. You'll only make it worse."

"Good job he never notices anything," murmured Isabel.

Or lets sleeping dogs lie, I thought.

A little later Malcolm got me into the garden on the pretext of helping him shift some logs. He cleared his throat, hesitated, and then asked awkwardly:

"Get on all right with Isabel, Mike?"

"Yes, fine, Mr Harper."

"Good." He hesitated again, as if he were floundering in some foreign language. "My wife," he said at length, ". . . very pleased she's got a young man, um, boy friend . . . doesn't make friends easily . . . sheltered life, you know . . . too sheltered, perhaps . . . difficult girl, no mistake . . . some queer hang-ups . . . not everyone'd be patient with her, know what I mean?"

"Oh, yes."

"Can't get through to her myself . . . no communication . . . I worry a bit, you know . . . highly-strung girl . . . just let loose, as you might say . . . girls' school a bit like a nunnery . . . getting a boy friend, put her in a bit of a spin . . . but she's a good girl, sure of that . . . bit of a responsibility for you, eh? . . . I mean, got to go careful with her, know what I mean?"

Know what I mean! He didn't know one-fifth of it. I was getting to like him, though. He really did mean to do right by everyone. But if he was like this in his business, his secretary must do all his talking for him.

"I understand, Mr Harper."

"Leads you a bit of dance sometimes, doesn't she?" he said, smiling.

I was sure he knew those footprints weren't his own, although what kind of dance Isabel and I could have performed in the garden, in the rain, during the small hours, must have puzzled him exceedingly. He was wise enough not to enquire.

It had surprised me how promptly Isabel had gone downstairs in answer to her mother's call. I'd have expected more defiance. It seemed that she was far more anxious to please her mother than she was prepared to admit. She despised all her values, and yet this weird bond remained. And between them was Malcolm. Behind his patient resignation I detected a hurt look. They both blamed him for coming between them, and he had no defence against either. I think he longed for Isabel to love him, but it was no use.

Later that morning the sun came out strongly, making Malcolm's wet garden dazzle, and Isabel and I paced about outdoors, talking the latest adventure over and over. Meanwhile Dr Diener, I supposed, would be just sitting around like a fisherman waiting for a bite, till we called on him again. But he had been more active than that. He had visited the college that Sunday, examined some archives in the library, roamed the grounds, and chatted up Jenny O'Brien.

"Why is he so interested in Jenny?" I asked Miss Dummer when we met that evening in the lounge of their hotel.

"Her views on art?" she suggested gravely.

"Are they relevant?"

"Nothing is irrelevant to the Herr Doctor."

When we told Dr Diener of the latest development, he removed his glasses and polished them, and a light kindled in his grey, very un-English eyes. "Two spirits," he observed, "dependent on each other. It gets, as Alice says, curiouser and curiouser. It is most interesting."

I had heard of surgeons who would gleefully call their colleagues round them to look at an unusually beautiful tumour. He reminded me of them. He must have read my thoughts, for he said:

"Come now, you would not expect a doctor to weep over a patient, would you? It will not help you in the least if I groan in sympathy with you. We must be more practical than that.

"We learn that there are two spirits. One is your *doppelgänger*, wishing to invade your person, and the other is this child-spirit, evidently wishing to be freed. As Michael has said, the child is becoming more and more distinct. What do we learn from this?"

He removed his glasses again and waggled them for emphasis. "Your *doppelgänger*," he said, "has been prompted by some force in your college to haunt Michael and attack you through him. Yet in the spirit world, it seems, risks must be taken in order to succeed, just as in ours. The more daring its raids become, the more it risks losing everything; the nearer it gets, the nearer the spirit of the captive child gets. The child can haunt too, it can make itself known; it can intervene, as it did when Michael drew your picture."

"It's crying for help," protested Isabel.

"And what help does it require? We may infer—" he hesitated, and repeated: "We may *infer* that the two spirits need to be separated. Then, perhaps, the child would be freed, and your *doppelgänger* would lose its hold on you."

"But what can we do about it?" demanded Isabel.

Miss Dummer, who had been watching over us all, anxious as a mother hen, broke out urgently:

"*Es wäre eben zehr gefährlich!*"

"Miss Dummer says, it is dangerous," said the doctor, "and indeed it may be;—as dangerous as plucking a cub from a lioness. Yet, as I have said, your *doppelgänger* makes mistakes. Perhaps it will make a decisive one."

"How should we know if it did?" I asked.

"Reason would suggest," said Dr Diener, "that all its appearances are failures of a kind. It—she—is 'spotted' like an unsuccessful burglar, or detected like an unsuccessful spy. She is most dangerous when invisible, when she is, as it were, brain-washing you."

"So we should make her show herself?"

"To advise that would place me under a grave responsibility; and yet, yes, that would follow."

Miss Dummer shuddered.

"Let's go over it just once more," said Isabel.

"You're like Dr Diener," I said. "All, right then."

We sat on our bench in the cemetery and once again I parroted a synopsis of the gospel according to Dr Diener. Isabel had projected a spirit-image of herself which some alien spirit had captured and used ever since to keep in touch with her. While it kept its prisoner, the said alien spirit had the power to reproduce Isabel's appearance, except, for some reason, the eyes, which it hid behind black glasses. It needed to make its "home" in a human body, and had fixed on Isabel as its object, but it could not force her to be its hostess against her will. So it selected a lover for Isabel (enter Michael

Wilkinson) and tried to—what could I say?—seduce him, I suppose—with the intention of making him—as it were—impregnate her with itself. It could wait for years . . .

All of which seemed mad by daylight, and grotesquely out of place in our own world. We were not Minangkabauers nor members of the Kawiri tribe of Southern Borneo. Yet nothing else was important by comparison.

There was a new development. The captured child-spirit was crying for release . . .

"Yes: release from *what*?" said Isabel. "It's ghastly to hear it running about, lost and terrified."

She had changed. She was not worried about herself any more, but about the child. It was as if she had become a mother.

I tried to console her. "Look, Elizabeth needs the child . . . she mustn't harm it . . . it's got its own strength, anyway . . . it can stop her having all her own way . . ."

"It's crying for help," insisted Isabel. Then, with that familiar touch of hysteria: "I'll make Elizabeth show herself. Dr Diener says her appearances are failures . . . I'll force her . . . I'll confront her—"

"Calm down, now."

"I will. I'll draw a portrait of myself."

"That will be handing over to her completely."

"Yes, it will," she admitted, in despair.

Poor Isabel sat there at a loss, too white and tense for tears, and poor Mike sat beside her, perplexed, and longing to help her, and yet with a part of him marvelling that he had ever got involved with her.

We had reached a deadlock; but just at this moment we heard footsteps on the cemetery path, and we turned to see Miss Dummer, pinker than ever in the ruddy evening light, and slightly out of breath.

"Good evening," she said. "May I, excuse me please, join you?"

94

She sat down beside us, panting, a big, ungainly girl, nearly as tall as I and all of twenty pounds heavier, with a puddingy face and an ill-fitting frock that bunched in loops over her belt.

"I have all the way to the college walked already," she said, then frowned and corrected herself. "I have walked all the way to the college, no? In order," she explained, "to find you. You were, of course, not there. By chance I saw you as I returned past the church."

"What can we do for you, Miss Dummer?"

"The boot is on the other foot," said Miss Dummer patly. "I wish to help you."

"Yes, I know you do," said Isabel curiously. "I've watched your face while we've talked with Dr Diener. Why do you bother with us?"

"Eventually, because I think I can help where the Herr Doctor cannot."

"How's that?"

"Dr Diener," said Miss Dummer, "has said that education weakens the psychic powers. The Herr Doctor is a very learned man. He can expound, he can explain, but he cannot precisely help you, because he has buried his gift under his learning."

"We need a witch, like Jenny's grandmother," said Isabel. "But aren't you yourself very well educated too, Miss Dummer? You wouldn't be a witch, would you?"

"No, indeed. But in my part of Germany, Westphalia, is much folk-lore. The *doppelgänger* is a native of our region! That is, of course, joking. But—"

"Yes?"

Miss Dummer frowned. "Your English language," she said, unexpectedly, "is not exact. You have the word 'sympathy'. It is not exact. We have in German *das Mitgefühl*, the With-Feeling. This is exact. You must be one with this child. You must feel as it feels. You must, as it were, *be* it."

"So—?"

"You must use the Sympathetic Magic. Every detail must be exact. Even your *doppelgänger* has failed because she has not been enough exact! We must make a plan."

"Then what, Miss Dummer? A séance?"

"*Séance* I do not like. It is a French word, and the French language is not exact . . . but yes, a séance of a kind."

"Is it dangerous, Miss Dummer?"

"I am afraid so. Or we defeat the *doppelgänger* utterly, or perhaps we help her. Yes, there is danger. It is as if there are two bottles, one full of good medicine, one full of poison. We do not know which is which. We take one—we take a chance."

"You don't mind taking it, Miss Dummer?"

"It is the professional pride. I cannot let a contemptible evil spirit insult a client."

The light was dying in the cemetery, and the chill of evening was setting in. Miss Dummer stood up. "I must now return. Do nothing till we meet again. You wish we should consult together, no?"

"Yes," said Isabel warmly, "we wish we should consult together."

"Good, then tomorrow we arrange a meeting."

Isabel gripped her arm. "You're good value, Miss Dummer."

"Please?"

"I mean you're a friend. Thank you."

Miss Dummer smiled. "*Bitte schön*," she said.

14 After being away from it for a day and a half, I found college faintly strange, and rather drab, as your old belongings seem when you've just opened your Christmas presents. As for my own home, not seen for three weeks, it might have belonged in some previous existence. However, there was a letter from my mother, to whom I had written during the week mentioning that I was going to the Harpers' for the week-end. This news had so excited my father that he actually put in a few lines of his own as a postscript:

"You certainly get in with the best people, chum!" (By calling me this, he aimed to bridge the generation gap.) "This new mate of yours is none other than *the* Malcolm Harper of Harper's Ltd! Quite apart from that empire, he happens to have his finger in one or two big advertising agencies, too! If you should hear him mention that he wants a Managing Director for one of them, don't forget your old dad, will you? . . ."

Jokes are meant.

"Yes," said Isabel, when I told her this. "Well, I'm *the* Isabel Carrick. *Not* Harper."

"Do you remember your real father at all?"

"No, all I can remember is a sort of background din. I wish I did."

"Maybe you're better off as it is."

"Yes," said Isabel ruefully, "I expect I get my own nasty

nature from him. Have you told your mother I'm one of the Gorgon sisters?"

"She says," (I consulted the letter) " 'Isabel sounds very nice'."

"Yes, I am," said Isabel inconsistently and belligerently. "I'm not a difficult girl with queer hang-ups, as that idiot Malcolm told you. I'm a nice, ordinary girl who happens to be a hat-rack for the hang-ups of weirdos from Another World. Which, unfortunately, makes me a weirdo too—"

"Calm down," I said. "You're all right—what's the matter?"

A tear was glistening in her eye. Malcolm had been so right when he said, "Got to go careful with her, know what I mean?" Whenever she spoke in this jokey pugnacious way, it was a sign that she was near tears.

"I'm daft," she said, sniffing crossly. "It's just that whenever I talk about my real father, it makes me weepy."

I'd never have guessed it. This was another side to her.

Jenny was back, looking rosier and healthier than ever, but, for all her brisk, rather teachery manner, oddly on edge.

"One week to go, Michael," she said, "and then you'll forget all about Newfield Abbey and all of us here, won't you?"

"Never, Jenny."

" 'Never Jenny'! You do sound ominous. No more Sights while I've been away, I hope?"

"Yes, as a matter of fact." I wasn't going to stand there tamely letting her get at me. "Some very strange things have happened."

Whereupon, like some ruthless counsel in court, she got the whole story out of me. I spoke reluctantly, even shamefacedly, but I told her everything, except for the detail of her sleepwalking. She listened darkly, her mouth tightening.

"You just want to believe it all, don't you, Michael?"

"Jenny," I said (I surprised myself how patient I was being), "Jenny: Dr Diener himself believes what we've told him."

"Dr Diener," said Jenny, "is a great psychiatrist. He knows exactly what he is doing."

"You think he's just humouring us?"

"Yes. Going along with you, to see what's motivating you."

"Jenny, don't you see that you twist the facts to suit yourself, just as much as you say I do?"

"But you prefer to listen to his secretary," she went on, ignoring this, "because she offers you some mumbo-jumbo from a Bavarian village."

"Jenny, why do you get so uptight about it?"

"Tampering with the occult is dangerous," she replied, glaring.

I looked at her in amazement. She was flushed, and the pupils of her eyes were so dilated that their green had turned black.

"And I don't mean that you're likely to be carried off by the fairies," she snapped. "I mean that it can be very very destructive psychologically. 'No chamber is so haunted as the chamber of the mind.'"

"That's very good, Jenny," I said, mildly. "Is it your own?"

In an instant she was all charm again. She flashed me her disarming grin. "As a matter of fact, I read it on the back of a paperback book of ghost stories." She lowered her voice and spoke very earnestly. "Michael, you're an artist. Artists are very susceptible, vulnerable people; even a bit lunatic, if the truth were told. Just read a few biographies if you doubt that. I don't want your art to sink to creative therapy inside a mental home, that's all."

"Why should you worry, Jenny?"

"Ah, well now, it's a soft spot I have for you, alanna, so I have."

99

No use defending myself with the rigmarole of my experiences. I had never met anyone so blindly obstinate.

"Thank you," I said.

"Well! Take care!"

Miss Dummer rang us up at lunch-time and arranged to meet us in the college's "Little Theatre", a conveniently secluded spot, that evening. Punctually on the stroke of eight she turned up. The surprise was that she had Dr Diener with her. It was rather like making a date with a girl, to find that she'd brought her mother along too.

"The Herr Doctor and I have consulted together," she announced. "I would not, of course, proceed without his approval."

No, of course not; how could we have supposed otherwise? "Do you believe in Sympathetic Magic then, sir?" I asked.

"The practices of simple folk-lore and those of modern psychiatry," he replied, "are often not far apart. Ancient man put great faith in dreams; so do psychiatrists. Psychiatrists will persuade a patient to talk about his buried fears and feelings of guilt. So does the oldest Christian church: they call it confession."

"This is a modern sort of spirit," I remarked. "It goes in for brain-washing and kidnapping."

"No, an ancient one," said Dr Diener. "Might not modern man have been taught such things by the powers of darkness?"

He removed his glasses and waved them at me. "Your dream is not an uncommon one," he said. "It speaks for itself. The frightened child is a symbol of insecurity; the great dark room and the ugly noise represent the outside world; the two dead bodies are the parents whose love the child believes it has lost. What is interesting is that the dream, which should be Isabel's, has been transferred to

Michael. Even more interesting is the fact that the dream is invading your waking life."

Miss Dummer was looking anxious. "Excuse me, Herr Doctor, too much intellectuality—"

"Yes, indeed. Miss Dummer insists that we should not reason too much in this matter. Reasoning weakens our instinctive powers. Excuse me, Miss Dummer. Please proceed."

"For the Sympathetic Magic," said Miss Dummer, "we have two needs. First, a symbol. You have heard how witches make waxen models of people, no?—and then stick pins in them? Yes, good. We shall not stick pins in our symbol, of course. We must, however, obtain one—a model, a picture—"

"Of the little girl?" I interrupted.

"Yes," said Miss Dummer, frowning slightly. "Our second need—"

"Well, as it happens, I—"

"One moment, please. Our second need is to re-enact a scene of much importance from Isabel's childhood. You have heard how the police reconstruct a crime, yes? Modern psychiatry will sometimes do the same." She smiled, and with conscious pride emitted another idiom. "There is nothing new under the sun! It is also good Sympathetic Magic, already."

"From my childhood?" said Isabel. "The bit where I broke the cup?"

"Yes, excellent."

"And we're to reconstruct that? Who's to be my mother?"

"I myself will take her part."

"Oh, Miss Dummer, you're not much like her!"

"No matter, we shall use the hypnosis."

"What?"

"Hypnotism," put in Dr Diener gently. "I use it with some of my patients."

"And where are we to do this?"

"The college atmosphere," said Miss Dummer, "is important. We shall enact the scene here. Perhaps in this room."

"And what about the symbol?"

I was bursting to say my piece about this. "I've got one," I said. "A photo, I mean. Isabel, aged three. It's in my suit pocket."

Astonishingly, I had forgotten about this from the moment I'd put it in my pocket, even though I'd worn that very suit the last week-end! They asked me to fetch it; and apprehensively I rose to do so. Outside, the light was failing.

Miss Dummer understood my reluctance. "I go with you," she said.

"We all will," said Dr Diener; and so, no doubt to the curiosity of anyone who saw us, we all trooped out to my chalet, obtained the photo, and returned to the Little Theatre. Elizabeth, who seemed not to like company, had not appeared.

We gathered round the table and studied the grave little face of Isabel, aged three.

"It may even be," remarked Dr Diener, "that your having this about you helped the child to get through to you. It is, of course, pure speculation—"

"Will it do for a symbol?" I asked.

"Better if a drawing were made of it," said Miss Dummer. "The creative act is most important in these cases."

"By me or by Isabel?"

"Better by Isabel."

I felt most uneasy. "And all this is very dangerous, Miss Dummer?"

"Oh, yes." She paused for a moment. "It is dangerous if it should go wrong."

"Can we guard against that?"

"Yes, by preparing everything correctly."

"By preparing everything correctly." And if we left something out through ignorance? I went about in dread. Nothing was happening: no dreams, no visitations, nothing; but the very hush was ominous.

A self-portrait was what Isabel dreaded most. Of course, this portrait was no longer "her double", but it was herself, and remembering what had happened to me when I had been induced to draw her, I trembled for her very soul.

We had fewer lectures this last week of the course, and spent a lot of time preparing for the final exhibition. Isabel did her portrait in the Art Room, surrounded by our fellow-students. I kept going over to look at it. She was turning the imperious-looking little black-haired beauty into a life-size head-and-shoulders. I could see her grown self in it, and her mother—she looked, I am afraid, very like her mother—and also, remotely, the likeness of someone else, I couldn't tell whom. This worried me, because the thing was so involved with mystery, not just a portrait but a Symbol, that I imagined psychic elements everywhere. However, the drawing was finished with no unnatural interference, and was admired by everyone.

It was brilliant. Isabel could draw character, somehow. The portrait had a personality which the little photo hardly hinted at. Several of the tutors came in to see it, and even Jenny was lost in admiration.

"You're an artist, girl," she said. "You really know yourself, don't you? At least," she added, "when you draw you do."

I could imagine what she would have said if she had known why Isabel was drawing it.

We agreed to leave the portrait with all the other students' gear in the cupboard in the exhibition hall. Terribly worried as to what might happen in the night, I even offered to spend it in her room. It would have been the most blameless night any couple could spend together, because we wouldn't dare risk doing what most couples would do; but Isabel, though she was lonely and frightened and strongly tempted, turned the offer down.

"It may be playing into her hands."

In fact, nothing at all happened that night, and once again we exchanged anxious whispers at breakfast; and no doubt our fellow-students again got the wrong idea. I was not reassured by the fact that nothing had happened. Jenny would have said it was because I didn't want to be. Whatever the case, I felt as if both Isabel and I were awaiting execution.

15 My O Level results were due, and I was expecting my mother to phone them to me. They had once seemed a matter of life or death, but I was now so consumed by the present crisis that I was practically indifferent to them.

It was Wednesday in the fourth and final week of the course. Isabel had finished her picture and we waited for Miss Dummer. We got through the day, behaving normally. Have you ever thought how, among the people you see behaving normally on a railway platform, or in a shop, or whatever, there may be someone contemplating suicide or murder, or being blackmailed? We bear our worries in an indifferent world. No one knew about us. We waited for Miss Dummer.

She, with typical thoroughness, had arranged it all. She told the gratified Principal that Dr Diener's researches into the college's past were now nearly completed, and that after a final meeting he would write a paper on them. She told us to meet herself and Dr Diener in the Little Theatre at eight o'clock, bringing the portrait with us.

The Little Theatre was on the first floor, just past the corridor that led to the tutors' rooms. It had a small, shallow stage, which you could enter from the back, and about twelve rows of chairs. Between the chairs and the stage was an area of floor space. Miss Dummer propped up the portrait on the stage, and switched on the footlights, so that the infant Isabel became haloed with coloured lights. She made us all sit in the front row facing it. This done, she sat with her head bowed as if in prayer.

We sat like this for several minutes, and I wondered glumly whether after all we might be making fools of ourselves. Isabel shifted her feet.

"When do we—"

"Sh'sh."

But she finished her question, with a touch of irritation:

"—enact the cup scene?"

"Sh'sh," said Miss Dummer again. "Not yet. Patience."

"But—"

Dr Diener, sitting to the left of her, laid his hand on hers. "Relax," he said, in a low, deep voice, so compelling that I, too, let myself go, with a long submissive sigh. "Relax, relax. Give in. Do not think. Relax."

He had such a soothing effect that I felt as if keys had been turned all over my body to slacken its wires. He spoke again, very quietly, but quite conversationally:

"One factor is missing, and we are waiting for it."

"Now," whispered Miss Dummer, "watch, please, the portrait, without ceasing."

More at ease, drowsily almost, we kept our eyes on the portrait. The footlights made it dazzle, and I began to see it in the centre of coloured rings. But nothing happened.

After some minutes Dr Diener said very quietly to Miss Dummer: *"Sie ist da, nicht?"*

"Oh, ja."

"She is there, isn't she?—Oh, yes." *She* was Elizabeth, presumably? They must be very keenly attuned, because I was the chosen of Elizabeth, and I could sense nothing.

Another wait. The coloured rings round the portrait were pulsing and flexing, and I lost sight of the picture itself. But I knew by now the wicked aura of Elizabeth and the pitiful appeal of the dream-child, and certainly neither of these was present.

My faith that anything at all would happen began to grow wan. Even Dr Diener himself seemed to be growing restless.

Miss Dummer whispered: *"Achtung."*

—and added: "She arrives."

There were slow, uncertain footsteps outside. They passed the door at the back of the room, through which we had entered, and faltered towards the door at the back of the stage. This door began to open with painful slowness. I turned my gaze from the portrait and blinked, and the coloured rings disappeared. Now I knew whom Dr Diener had meant when he said, "She is there." Into the footlights, blindly, came Jenny. She could not be sleepwalking so early in the evening, but she was obviously in some sort of trance. She came right to the edge of the stage and would have fallen had not Dr Diener gone swiftly up to take hold of her. She stopped at his touch and said in a voice rougher and much more strongly Irish than her normal one:

"Holy Mother of God."

Then, hoarsely, in a whisper, she echoed the question of Dr Diener:

"Is she here?"

"She will be, Jenny, now you have come."

There was an armchair on the stage, a piece of stage property, and he pulled it quickly forward and pushed her into it.

We all stood up and gathered round her. She lay back, the portrait beside her. Her eyes were closed.

Her eyelids began fluttering, very rapidly, like an insect's wings. Her eyes were turned up and she was showing the white of them, horribly. She began to moan and twitch.

"Relax," said Dr Diener again, in that masterful voice, so low, yet with the vibration of a gong, "relax, relax, relax . . ."

Jenny subsided, she positively crumpled, into the armchair, and lay back, her eyes wide open now, but unseeing, her face turned towards the ceiling.

"Good, good," said Dr Diener, as though he were soothing a small child. "Relax, relax. Good . . ."

Then he stood back and contemplated her. She seemed to be in a deep sleep. His shoulders dropped and he let out his breath. He turned to Miss Dummer with a small smile of triumph. Like a surgeon explaining his moves at an operation, he said to us, in a conversational whisper:

"This is your 'college atmosphere', this young lady."

"The Herr Doctor has for a long time suspected it," murmured Miss Dummer proudly.

"Do you not understand?" said the doctor. "Miss O'Brien is strongly psychic, a natural medium. She is extremely attractive to supernatural forces. She did not know it, but she is. The gift of her grandmother has jumped a generation."

Jenny, that intellectual sceptic, lay inert, serene and pale.

"And now," said Miss Dummer, "now we have all we require. Now we can begin."

Isabel, who was the reason for all this, had stayed back until now, like some star player leaving all the work to her handlers. Now she sat down in front of the portrait as though waiting to be crowned, or perhaps electrocuted: the central figure in the drama. The light from the footlights, reflected back, glowed on her face and hair. She looked slight and young and defenceless. She was not an enchanted princess, as I had called her once, but what she said she was, an ordinary girl who was caught up in an incredible problem. I was weak with hope and fear for her. I loved her.

She said quietly to Miss Dummer: "What are we going to do?"

"We shall liberate the child."

"Elizabeth will fight you."

"We are now very strong."

And very German, Miss Dummer. We have obeyed all the rules: nothing can go wrong!

Miss Dummer drew me back, and stood beside me in the fading light. Dr Diener knelt by Isabel's side. He held her hands and began to speak to her urgently, in a voice so low that I couldn't make out his words. He seemed to be repeating himself over and over again. Isabel's eyes, fixed on the portrait, opened to a wide and glassy stare. In a little while she began to whimper. This was almost more than I could bear. I wanted to throw my arms round her and protect her; but the solid form of Miss Dummer checked me. She held my arms, she shook her head gravely, and I held back.

Dr Diener picked up a cup or mug which he had hidden somewhere nearby, and with a sharp rap on the back of Isabel's chair, broke it.

Isabel began to cry. It was not her usual kind of crying, but in the puny tones of a very young child. She fell to her knees. Miss Dummer went to her quickly and quietly, and knelt before her.

Miss Dummer in the rôle of Isabel's mother had been beyond imagining. In fact, she did not attempt to act, but simply positioned herself in front of Isabel, a lay figure. Isabel reached out for her, blindly. Miss Dummer barred her embrace with crossed arms. Isabel broke into desperate sobs.

It was cruel, it was intolerable, but I knew I must not interfere. I forced myself to stare at the portrait. The daylight had all but failed by now and the footlights shone brighter, and the portrait throbbed and dazzled. Bands of light welled from it and burst before my eyes.

Jenny, supine and almost forgotten in her armchair, uttered a long, groaning sigh. She stirred, she rolled drunkenly from side to side. She began moaning. Dr Diener half-rose to go to her assistance. Miss Dummer, managing to be commanding, patient and dead calm all at once, said warningly:

"*Nein!*"

He knelt down again, submissively. The portrait glowed

with a livid white light of its own. In the next instant it became dark. The footlights, still glowing on the little group below the stage, seemed to shed no light on it. Jenny, with a long, deep, restful sigh, sank back again in her chair. A white vapour began to pour from her mouth and swirl about her face and body. It became compact; it resolved itself into coils in front of her.

Isabel knelt there subdued and tranquil. Miss Dummer put her arms round her, her hand behind Isabel's head, so that she stared over her shoulder. The ectoplasm, in writhing white serpents, began to disclose a form.

Like seeing a statue made by a miracle, I thought. I was no longer distressed. We had done it. We were bringing the child away.

The tiny form of Isabel, aged three, hung in the coiling ropes of vapour. More and more clearly was it defined. And now we heard its voice. It was the same little voice I had heard in my dream, that Isabel and I had heard in the garden, but it was hardly afraid any more. It wavered between doubt and joy. It sensed rescue.

Isabel drew away from Miss Dummer and held out her arms.

Miss Dummer whispered, "Wait, wait."

Wait. The little spirit hung in the balance between its world and ours, seen, heard, not yet to be reached.

Surely, surely we were there now.

I felt a sudden, terrible stab of misgiving. Jenny's limp body gave a sudden jerk. Isabel clutched Miss Dummer and began panting. The doctor started up. All three turned and looked at me.

There was no time, no world, a void. There was deep silence.

The two doors of the Little Theatre burst open with a noise like gunshot. A wind roared through the room. The portrait spun from the box against which Miss Dummer had propped it and whizzed over our heads to crash down among the chairs. The footlights went mad, zig-zagging and gyrating. Isabel screamed. The air was icy and pungent with evil. Between me and the others appeared the figure of Elizabeth. The footlights glittered on the hateful black discs.

I was adrift beyond time and space. I was no longer in the Little Theatre. I was nowhere definable at all. Elizabeth was before me in a void, like a portrait whose background has been filled in. I could remember that, as Isabel screamed, I had seen my own body fall down and that I now stood clear of it, but even this fragment of memory was dwindling like a fleeting dream. I felt no emotion except a strange, faint exhilaration. I was quite without fear.

Elizabeth smiled her blind smile. She was the exact image of Isabel and yet as different as anything in the realm of nature. It was not a difference merely between good and bad, or black and white, but an absolute difference, a difference between human and alien.

Elizabeth smiled. She spoke to me in that voice which was Isabel's voice and yet, also, inexpressibly different, as if sound, like vision, had been turned round in a mirror to its opposite.

"Join me, Michael."

To hear my name spoken in that voice was a sweet, aching, terrible thrill. Our scientific age has lost touch with some kinds of knowledge. Those tales of seductive mermaids and alluring witches and *femmes fatales* are not all childish make-believe. They have grown from some core of truth.

"You have awakened from a bad dream, Michael. Life is a bad dream. Leave it, leave it. Life is chaos. Leave it. Join me, Michael."

She moved nearer.

"I love you, Michael, and you love me. You think you love her only because she is like me. Join me."

What had I to lose? I was in her world now, but whatever happened, I would still be Michael. Wherever you go, you take yourself with you.

Elizabeth smiled and held out her arms. When she did that, I was reminded of the arms of Isabel as she had stretched them out to the child. It recalled "the bad dream", the world I had left. I was no longer adrift. I heard a far-off confusion of voices. It was like the row outside the great room in my dream, but it soon ceased to be an uproar of nothing and became articulate. I heard the voices of Miss Dummer and Isabel, and the Irish voice of Jenny Holy Mothering and muttering in her trance. The voices "scrambled", as when the phone is jammed. The voices overlaid one another and clashed and gibbered.

Then I heard the voice of the child. It was between me and Elizabeth, running frantically about, panting and whimpering. It began sobbing, out of control, the sobs ricochetting from Elizabeth to me. It held Elizabeth back. Her voice rose and sharpened.

"Join me, Michael, Michael . . ."

But from in front of her I heard another voice: "Michael, Michael, Michael . . ."

I was torn between these two tongues, the serpentine insistence of Elizabeth and the pleading of the child. Elizabeth ceased to cajole me. Her voice became haggish.

"You cannot have her. Never. She is mine. She is my little dog. She is my eyes."

I understood. I went slowly forward, past the unseen, hysterical child, and held out my arms. I reached Elizabeth, and, as she smiled triumphantly and went to embrace me, I struck the black glasses from her eyes.

I had a momentary glimpse of their hellish glitter. They were not blind, but too evilly brilliant for our world. If I had been inside my own body they would surely have killed me, but my naked spirit faced her, and it could not be killed.

She swung away from me with a wail of rage and despair. I heard the wracked sobbing of the child as I abandoned it. There was a sensation like being in a lift that has come loose from its cable, there was a kick in my heart and a blinding throb in my temples, and I rejoined my body, and came back again to the human world of chaos and dream.

The four of them were grouped round me on the floor. I heard one of the Little Theatre doors knocking gently in a draught. I sat up, quite calm, and quite empty, feeling nothing. I gazed round at them: Jenny white and dazed, Isabel weeping, Dr Diener grave and intent, and Miss Dummer tragically worried.

"It failed, didn't it?" I said.

"Never mind now—"

"It failed, didn't it?"

Dr Diener nodded. "We lost the little girl."

"I could not hold her," said Jenny, humbly and brokenly.

"Something was lacking," said Miss Dummer piteously. "All was prepared. There was some detail we omitted. This I do not understand."

"Are you all right?" I asked Isabel.

She nodded, sniffing and rubbing her face with the back of her hand. "I thought you were dead."

"So did I," I said. "I've some things to tell you—"

"Not now," said Dr Diener, restraining me. "Later. Keep quiet now."

Till you're in a state to record it, I thought cynically. It's an ill wind. What a fascinating appendix for his book all this would make.

Isabel said: "Yes, the séance failed, Mike, and we'll never try it again. Or anything like it. Not ever."

16 What I said just then about Dr Diener was unfair. He spent a full hour with me afterwards, letting me talk, and by the end of it I felt remade and able to face the world. After this he talked to Isabel and after that, late into the night, I think, to Jenny. Whatever fees he charged his paying customers, he was worth them. He restored your self-esteem.

Even so, I felt like a plaice on a slab. Flat. It was all over. My mother rang up next morning and elatedly told me that I had passed all my O Levels. I had worried her silly for a whole year over my O Levels, but now they didn't matter.

"Oh, good," I said listlessly.

"Dad's so pleased."

"Is he? Good."

"*You* are pleased, aren't you?"

"Oh yes."

"Michael, is anything wrong? You haven't fallen out with your Isabel, have you?"

"No, of course not."

"M'm," said my mother, in a tone which suggested that she understood me to have said yes. "Well, that's all right then, isn't it? We'll see you on Saturday."

My mother was prophetic. I hadn't spoken to "my Isabel" yet, but when she drew me aside after breakfast I saw decision in her face, and my heart sank.

I had not told her yet of my last encounter with Elizabeth.

When the doors of the Little Theatre burst open, she had seen her appear and then disappear, and she had seen me pass out. She had no idea of what had happened next, but all the same her mind was made up.

"We can't go on together."

"Don't you love me?"

"You know I do. I'll never love anyone else, because I shan't let myself. I'll pretend I've gone into a nunnery. Girls younger than I have gone into nunneries. I mean it, Mike. You know why. We can't go on."

"But we must, we must. We're—we're soul-mates."

"No, Elizabeth is the soul-mate. She can destroy us."

"You said she'd never let us part!"

"I did, but now we're going to. She can't beat me if I don't let her, but I can't protect you as well."

"What am I supposed to do?"

"Leave me, and she'll leave you. You're no use to her without me."

"I can't live without you," I said.

"You'll have to, because you certainly can't live with me. Oh, Mike, think. Hasn't this month been terrible? How long do you think you can go on like this? Can't you see she'll ruin you?"

"I'm willing to risk that."

"You don't mean that. Not really. Anyway, I mean this. I know now that I can never really get rid of her, and so I shall learn to live with her. I'm privileged, as Jenny's always pointing out," said Isabel bitterly. "I'll never want for money and I can draw very nicely. She even boosts my drawings, aren't I lucky? I shall manage, and you must manage too."

"What about the little girl?" I said desperately.

"I knew you'd say that." Isabel paused, and then said, in that strangely old-fashioned way she sometimes had: "Don't you see? She is myself, and for some reason all this is a judgement on me."

"You are determined to be a martyr, aren't you?" I said, angry and wretched.

"Think so if you like. Last night was too awful, and I can't face it again. It's too dangerous. It was awful."

"Oh, *Isabel*—"

"No, Mike, don't. We've got three more days here and then we finish. Nothing more will happen now. I just know it won't. You'll be safe away from me. Get another girl friend."

"There'll never be anyone else."

"That's what they all say. No, don't, Mike. You know I'm right. See you in the Art Room."

And Isabel walked away without any sentimental goodbyes, without even thanking me; and quite rightly, because any lapse into emotion would have been disastrous. She'd "given me up" before, you'll remember, but that time it had been all gazing soulfully into each other's eyes and wallowing in our misery, and we soon got back together again; but this time she was as decisive as a surgeon's knife. And good for her. It was brave.

I didn't go to the Art Room, but I'm pretty sure she didn't either, because she wasn't to be seen all day. No doubt she kept to her room, where, I expect, the stiff upper lip quivered a bit.

As for me, I went to my chalet and lay on my bed and shed the bitterest tears of all my life. Then I got up, washed my face, locked up my feelings, and reviewed the last four weeks. I even managed to make a sick joke of the thought of Elizabeth scrambling around, in whatever abyss she inhabited, searching for her lost glasses. Then I thought about the future. One thing I could do was write all this down in a book, and, as you see, I did. I also decided that to stop feeling sorry for myself, the thing to do was to concern myself with other people. Upon which I sought out Jenny.

"The Ancient Greeks used to say 'Know Thyself'," said Jenny. "I could have used that advice, couldn't I?"

"You must have had a shock."

"You can say that again. Psychic all my life, and I've never known it! Dr Diener says that the migraines were probably due to that. Repression. One shouldn't deny one's own nature.

"Actually, when the real thing comes along, there's no question of denying it. When you all got to work in front of that portrait, it was like a magnet drawing me. I had no more chance of resisting than you could stop yourself in the middle of a fall."

"You were Miss Dummer's ace of trumps, Jenny. You and the portrait and the scene with the cup—it was going to be the winning combination. She forgot that Elizabeth made use of you too. Elizabeth's stronger than they thought."

"No," said Jenny. "Something was missing."

"What do you mean?"

"I don't know." Jenny reflected. "You see, the child was getting through at last. I knew Elizabeth was there, but she was weakening. The child was getting away from her, getting *through*. It was like giving birth. Said she, never having done so," added Jenny. "And then, when I'd nearly delivered her, something that should have been there wasn't."

"What sort of thing?"

"Impossible to say. It was like being stranded on the stage when someone fails to come in on cue. I went to pieces, and Elizabeth rushed into the gap."

"Yes. Well, that's that."

"Oh? So my career as a medium is over already, is it? If we knew what was missing we could do it."

"We never will. Isabel's dead set against it."

"We might manage without her."

"Oh, come on, Jenny, she's rather important in this situation! She *is* the situation!"

"I don't know . . . I don't know that she is, altogether." Jenny shook her head, frowning. "There's something else . . ."

"What happened to the portrait?" I asked suddenly.

"Ah, I've got that. Isabel wanted us to burn it. I couldn't allow that. I made her give it to me. It's in my room."

"God, Jenny. Aren't you a bit nervous of it?"

"Oh, more than a bit. But if I've inherited my grandmother's gift I ought to face such challenges, shouldn't I?" Jenny saw the expression on my face and laughed. "Yes, I know what you're thinking. I'm like some Bolshie who discovers she's a duchess. Anyway, if that little girl in the picture needs me again, she'll know where I am."

17 The next day, the last Friday of the course, was not too bad. I kept busy, and told myself that life must go on, although I had forgotten why. Isabel spoke to me very little, and when she did, was ridiculously polite and friendly. I wanted to tell her that if she went on acting like this, she'd end up just like her mother, and that nothing could be worth that; but it was no longer my business.

But Saturday, the day of the exhibition, looked like being awful. My parents turned up, my mother agog to meet Isabel and my father agog to meet Malcolm. I had to introduce everybody, of course. Isabel was perfectly charming, and all that that implies. If I hadn't known the cause of it, she would have made me sick. But she charmed my father all right. He was determined to be charmed.

"I say, Mike, she's a smasher, isn't she? You want to hang on to her!—Isn't she a lovely girl?" he appealed to my mother.

"Ye-es," said my mother judicially. She was far less ready to be captivated without a struggle by Malcolm Harper's heiress. "Yes, very nice . . . She seems rather *old* for Michael, don't you think?"

"Oh, girls grow up more quickly than boys. Nothing wrong with that."

"No-o . . ."

"I think she's a smasher," said my father doggedly.

"M'm'm . . . Her *clothes* surprise me," said my mother.

119

"Michael gave me the impression that she was a bit of a rebel . . . You know, anti-parent, like so many of them . . . She certainly hasn't joined the dress-revolution, has she? No shapeless jumper and scruffy jeans about *her* . . ."

"No, she says that's really being conventional," I said sullenly, hating all this. "She doesn't think it's revolutionary to be just like everyone else."

"No, of course not," said my father stoutly. "You sound as if you're trying to put him off, when he's obviously fallen for her in a big way and quite right too!"

"I don't doubt she's very nice," said my mother. But she was no more ready to accept Isabel at first sight than she would have bought the first dress shown her in a shop.

Jenny was my only comfort in all this.

"Come on, Michael. It's not the end of the world."

"Yes it is."

"Nonsense. Do you think you've been playing some holiday game, timed to last four weeks? You're not finished yet."

"Yes I am."

"Like to bet?"

What made things worse was that I had to stand the mateyness of the Harpers as well, and, of course, their fraternizing with my parents. In that field my mother did rather well, letting Mrs Harper do all the scoring, pretending to be impressed, and acting so modestly that she seemed to have a card or two up her sleeve, and I think Mrs Harper lost her nerve a bit. But Malcolm listened to my father deferentially and put in only a shy, occasional word; and my God, my father talked his head off and oversold himself. It was terrible.

I was dreading that he would invite the Harpers to lunch at The Three Feathers and insist on paying for everything. But luckily the Principal had already invited them to lunch as distinguished (and paying) guests, so we went to the college canteen, and paid about one-tenth as much for a meal about one-half as good. I had no appetite, and my mother noticed it, and kept plying me with sneaky little questions about Isabel, and whether everything was all right between us.

We went back to the exhibition. I had reached the depths of gloom and wanted nothing but to pack up and go home, but my father insisted on hanging about, on the pretext of looking round again, although he'd already seen everything several times over.

I took my place resignedly by my own exhibits. And then, just as the Harpers came back into the room, I heard the whimpering of the child again. Amid the giant buzz of the visitors' voices I heard it inside my head, and nothing would shut it out.

I looked across to Isabel's stand, but the room was so packed that I could not even see her. Perhaps this was a private experience, like my first dreams. I stood swaying on my feet and wondering what to do about it, and then Jenny came in from the corridor and confronted me.

"I must speak to you. At once."

She drew me into the corridor.

"Fetch the portrait down."

She might as well have asked me to fix a bomb.

"But Jenny—"

"Michael, don't argue. Hurry."

There was a half-mad stare in her eyes that scared me. Inside my head the weak clamour of the child persisted like a bird in a cage. I followed Jenny as she rushed upstairs to her room. She thrust the portrait, grimed but intact, into my hands.

"Now do exactly as I say. Fix it on your stand. Bring Isabel's parents over to see it. Tell them you've been called away—make any excuse. Come back to me here. And hurry, hurry, hurry."

"Yes, Jenny."

"Dad," I said, battling my way through the ranks and grabbing his elbow, "Dad, do something for me—*now*, Dad—"

He was astonished by all this drama, and you couldn't blame him, but he was only too ready to do what I asked, and even as I dashed out into the corridor I glimpsed him propelling the Harpers towards my stand.

"O.K., Jenny," I reported, panting.

"Mother of God," she said, "let's hope they don't walk away from it too soon. Is Isabel with them?"

"No."

"No matter. She will be." She held her brows. She was the colour of cream cheese and her pupils were so dilated that her eyes shone black. "Holy Mother . . ."

She swayed slightly and I caught hold of her. "Shall I call Dr Diener, Jenny?"

"No, no time . . . Stay here . . ."

She sank back on to her bed, a divan, out of place in this high-ceilinged part of the old mansion. "Michael," she said, "one of those two down there is the missing one . . . the one we needed at the séance . . ."

I did not understand, but I couldn't question her. I knelt by her side, still holding her arms.

"This time," she whispered, ". . . may . . . work . . ."

Her voice grew fainter as she spoke, and expired altogether. The voice of the child within my head had also expired. I felt it—oh, how can I explain this?—I felt its spirit drawn down my arms and out through my hands by the psychic power of Jenny. She was like a powerhouse, like a telephone exchange, like a nervous plexus. She connected the spirit world with ours, and though I knew only dimly what was going on, I sensed that it was going right.

I went to the window and drew the curtain against the afternoon light. I knelt by her again and took her hand, but she was beyond my contact now. She was white and inert,

122

and for one awful moment I thought that by letting go my hold on her just then I had let her die. But she stirred and murmured, her lips curved into a smile, and her eyes opened wide and green and radiant. She said, in a soft and heavy brogue:

"Come now, acushla . . ."

And then the voice of the child, not in a word, but a cry of passionate relief.

Jenny rolled slightly and uttered a deep, deep sigh.

I saw a shimmering mist drift across the room to the door. I went quickly out into the corridor and there, for a matter of seconds, I saw the image of a tiny girl in a glow of light. I watched her descend the stairs towards the lower corridor; and then, like a burst bubble, she was there no longer.

I went back to Jenny. She smiled at me dreamily from the bed.

"Was it a pretty child?"

"Beautiful, Jenny," I said.

"Go down, then. I'll come later."

I went out into the corridor again, and at the end of it, opposite the stairs, I saw Elizabeth. I had visualized the scene when the child was taken from her. I had imagined a witch writhing in the flames of hell. It was nothing like that. There was no fury, no hatred, no power. She was faint, like a ghost. She was drifting apart, as though a wind were blowing her to nothing. She dissolved before my eyes, and before I could even cry out, she was gone. I never saw her again.

I went, trembling, back to the exhibition room. I didn't know what to expect. What I found couldn't have been more ordinary. My parents and the Harpers were still grouped in front of the portrait, but they were no longer looking at it. My father was subjecting Malcolm to some of his inexhaustible chattiness and the two women were talking to each other.

And then Isabel threaded her way through the visitors and came up to Malcolm. Her face was all alive and happy. She looked as if she had stepped out of some spiritual bath. She smiled at him and said affectionately:

"Seen enough art for one day?"

He looked at her in wonder.

"Oh, no, no—it's very interesting—"

"You'd rather it were a flower-show, though, wouldn't you? Actually, the gardens here are pretty good." She took his arm and kissed him. "Come on, I'll show you round."

"What about your stand?"

"It'll keep. Come on."

And, arm-in-arm with him, she led him out of the room.

"Do my eyes and ears deceive me?" exclaimed Mrs Harper. "That's the first time she's kissed him in her life!"

But my eyes were opened. I had seen Isabel's face as she kissed Malcolm, and now I looked at the portrait, and I saw just who it was I had dimly recognized in it. The new spirit that had been added to Isabel, or rather the old one that had come back after being so long away, had brought out the likeness in her. She was not Isabel Carrick. She was Isabel Harper.

18 It was all right between Isabel and me. More than all right.

No, of course I didn't tell her that I had guessed Malcolm was her real father. That was for her and her family to discuss in their own good time. As a matter of fact, it was hard to talk to her about the events of the past month at all. She was in hilarious high spirits and seemed not only to want to avoid discussing them, but even, in an odd way, to have stopped believing in them. She wished to take her new happiness for granted.

I did joke her, very mildly, about her changed attitude to Malcolm.

"Well, I looked at him standing there, all patient, and I remembered how patient he'd always been, and I decided I loved him."

I remarked that it was a woman's privilege to change her mind, and left it at that.

I did confide in Jenny. We discussed the case of Isabel's mother.

"Well, of course, she would still have been living with her first husband when Isabel was conceived, and she might not have been able to tell for certain who the father was. There were one or two bad girls in County Mayo who couldn't possibly have named the fathers of their children . . . Still, I shouldn't think Mrs Harper was quite like them . . ."

Well, I suggested, perhaps she did know, and was afraid to

tell. Fear of her first husband, perhaps, and fear of her own mother (who, as Isabel had said, "went mad" over her divorce) and then, later, fear of how Isabel herself would take it. And mixed up with all this fear, maybe, the overriding fear of not being respectable, which was probably the strongest force in her life.

And what about Dr Diener and his theories?

Yes, we gave him full marks. Well, nearly full marks. Isabel *did* project a spirit-image of herself when she was an infant, which not only got no response from her mother, but—Dr Diener hadn't worked this out—was lost to her true father as well.

"But mind you," I said, "we don't know much about the spirit world, and we won't get much further by thinking about it. Miss Dummer's right about too much intellectuality."

"I should know," said Jenny.

I went down to the Harpers' for the next week-end. Isabel, I learned, had spent most of the week gardening, and had never left Malcolm's side.

"I think I'll have a go at flower-painting," she said to me. "It'll be a change from gargoyles, won't it?"

"You have had an amazing effect on her, Michael," Mrs Harper confided in me. "She's—well, I'm sure you can see for yourself. She's transformed. It's like a miracle."

She smiled at me, her real smile, not her social one. I didn't think I would ever like Mrs Harper's standards, but I might not be able to help liking Mrs Harper. I won't say that her nature had changed, but she had turned another side of it outwards, as the earth turns another face to the sun.

"The course did us both good," I said. "It was a good course."

"Yes, it seems to have been excellent. We've agreed that she shall go back there next term as a full-time student."

I went out to join Isabel and her father in the garden. Her mother stood watching me as I climbed the grass terraces. I glanced back at her and then at the pair above me, and I felt a sense of harmony I had never known elsewhere, ever, with anyone. Love had entered this home, and I was glad to have had a part in it, because although a lot is said, written and sung about love, I don't really think there's all that much of it about.